Lady Avery and the False Butler

Merry Spinsters, Charming Rogues

Sofi Laporte

Chapter One

THERE WAS SOMETHING ODD ABOUT THE BUTLER.

Lady Avery Heywood was standing on the doorstep of her brother's townhouse in Wimpole Street, bidding farewell to the servants. As she extended her slender gloved hand to Jerkins, she paused.

She'd seen Jerkins every day for the past seven years and had never noticed anything unusual about him. In fact, she'd barely even noticed he existed.

Butlers tended to have that effect. They faded into the background like an item in the house inventory— always there, providing a service when needed, but otherwise remaining unseen, like the clock in the hall that one never really noticed but would sorely miss if it were suddenly gone, or the mahogany sofa in the drawing room with its gaudy dolphin feet and nautical carvings. It was hideous, but no one gave it a second thought; one just accepted its presence.

Butlers were similar in that regard, for one could never quite remember what they looked like.

Avery, therefore, found it exceedingly odd that after all those years, she noticed that behind those metal-rimmed spectacles perching on his eagle nose, Jerkins the butler had breathtakingly beautiful eyes.

Smoky grey with a dark rim, fringed with thick black lashes that curled in a decadently feminine way. Not at all in character for a butler.

Her breath took a slight hitch.

For heaven's sake. 'Twas not the thing to wax poetic about a butler's eyes! Especially when one was about to bid him farewell forever.

Besides, many men had beautiful eyes, so why not Jerkins, too?

It wasn't that, really. It was more that, for the first time, she realised he was not just a butler, but goodness! A man.

Who could have known?

A man who looked at her with strange intensity. Almost as if he were...sad?

No. He couldn't be.

Regretful?

Whatever for?

When he took her slender, gloved hand in his large one, he crushed it so firmly, she feared her bones would crack. Just as she was about to remark on it, he let go.

She'd shaken everyone's hand. Mrs Billings, the housekeeper, Susy, the parlour maid, even footman Jim. She owed it to them, especially since her brother and his family had left a minute earlier without as much as bidding goodbye to any of them. They'd hurried past the quick succession before Selena announced she'd had enough and locked the door between the two master bedrooms.

Avery had cared for their ailing mother, who'd never got over her husband's early death, and after her passing, had moved in with her brother. She'd raised their boys since Selena was too preoccupied with her social life.

Avery hadn't minded. Really, she hadn't. Even though Selena had made it clear at every opportunity that she was a burden.

Taming four lively boys had given purpose to her life, and she'd hardly known a moment of boredom.

But now her life was about to become very, very quiet as she moved to the countryside to take care of Great-Aunt Euphemia, who was deaf and blind—and in all likelihood older than a mummy.

Before Avery knew it, she'd be old and withered herself.

She sighed.

As the carriage rattled through Hounslow Heath, she almost wished something would happen. The carriage could lose a wheel. A terrible storm could delay her journey. Or better still, a highwayman might stop them and kidnap her, and a great adventure would await her. He would have smoky, steel-grey eyes with a dark rim and curling eyelashes.

The highwayman, that is.

He would be dashing and handsome.

He'd have a horse. Like Dick Turpin's black mare. He would swing her onto it, and they would gallop across the heath in the moonlight. Her long gown would flutter in the wind, as would her long tresses of fiery red hair...

Avery knocked on the wall of the coach. "Stop. Stop the carriage immediately."

The carriage came to a halt.

She scrambled out of the coach and stood by the side of the road, gazing longingly over the heath. Perhaps there, where the grassland stopped, behind yonder cluster of brambles, bushes and trees, a highwayman was hiding ...

"It's an unfortunate place to stop, milady." The coachman swung from his seat and stood beside her.

"Because of highwaymen, I know." Avery let her eyes roam over the landscape.

"Nah. With the last of 'em swinging nearly ten years ago, I daresay the scourge of the highwaymen has finally been eradicated. They belong to another age. Our coaches are faster, and the roads have never been better and safer than they are now." The coachman helped himself to some snuff.

Avery gave him a curious look. "The last of them swinging—you mean Jax Tyrrell?"

Jax Tyrrell was a legend. Dangerous, dashing, and deadly. And very, very handsome.

Or so they said.

"Aye. The most famous of 'em all. Saw him swing meself all those years ago."

"Did you, now?" She turned to him with an inquisitive expression on her face.

"Aye. At Tyburn. Was the last hanging there before they moved the gallows to Newgate. 'Twas a massive

Chapter Two

Dusk had fallen when the carriage arrived at her brother's townhouse in Wimpole Street. The house already looked deserted as the windows were dark and the shutters drawn. Avery bade the coachman goodbye, then clutched her tapestry bag tightly and knocked.

She prayed someone was still there. What if Jerkins had already shut the house and all the servants were gone? What would she do then?

She pulled the bell again, then hammered on the door.

Nothing.

If all else failed, she could go to the back of the house to the garden side, attempt to make her way up and over the fence, and see if she could get in through a window on the ground floor.

She was ready to execute that plan when she heard a key turn. The door opened.

"Thank heavens you're still here, Jerkins," Avery breathed.

"Lady Avery." Jerkins stared at her as if she were Jax Tyrrell's ghost seeking penance. "Good heavens. Has there been an accident? Are you well?"

"I am well. Please let me in."

"Certainly."

The house was dark, and Jerkins had placed an oil lamp on the table in the hall.

Avery breathed a sigh of relief. "No accident. Nothing happened. I just decided not to leave. Not just yet. I want to stay a little longer, before, before...Anyway, it is of no consequence. Don't let me keep you, Jerkins. If you need to leave, please do. In fact, it is quite all right if you do. I can manage on my own." She clasped her hands tightly.

There was a pause as Jerkins studied her face. "I have no intention of leaving, my lady."

"You don't? But surely you are to go to Penmaron Hall? Have the other servants left?"

"Yes, indeed."

Avery rubbed her temples. "Then please explain why you are still here."

"Because there is still work to be done here. The house needs to be cleared before it can be returned to the landlord."

"I see." She furrowed her brows and tilted her head aside. "But you intend to do this work all on your own?"

"Indeed." A slight frown crossed his face. "My lady appears fatigued. May I suggest that your ladyship retires, and I'll serve a light repast anon."

Her face lit up. "That would be lovely. Bring it to the study, if you please."

Chapter Three

Someone pulled the curtains vigorously aside, allowing sunlight to flood the room.

"Time to get up, my lady."

Avery buried her face in the pillow and wished she were dead. Her head had turned into an anvil and ten blacksmiths were pounding on it with iron hammers. Bam-bam-bam!

"It is a bright and cheerful day. The sun is shining, and the sky is blue."

"Go to blazes, Jerkins."

"Certainly, my lady. Before I do, may I suggest you have some good strong coffee, bacon and eggs, toast, and kidneys?"

Avery groaned. "Don't talk to me about food."

"Indeed. I would have recommended some chops and liver, but as we're short of staff now, the others already having left for Penmaron Hall, I haven't been able to send Jim to the butcher's."

It took her several minutes to understand what he

was saying. He was a dark outline standing in front of the windows, and she squinted against the sunlight. Then she realised he was looking at her, and she pulled the blanket up to her chin.

"Jerkins. You do realise you're in my bedroom, don't you?"

"Yes, my lady, that is a fact that would be rather difficult to overlook." He stepped up to her bed and held a glass filled with a milky substance under her nose. "Drink."

Avery sniffed. "What is it?"

"Buttermilk, cornflour, salt and pepper."

"Faugh, that sounds horrid."

"It's called Scottish Fling, and it's an ancient remedy for hangovers."

"Hangover? I don't have a hangover." She winced as her head pounded anew.

"Yes, you do. You nearly emptied half a bottle of whisky last night."

"Terrible stuff." She shuddered as she took the glass. "I can't imagine why I'd ever want to drink whisky, let alone half a bottle." She brought the glass to her lips, then paused. "Oh. I remember now. It's because it's my birthday."

"Many happy returns, my lady."

"Go to blazes."

"Yes, my lady. I believe you already consigned me there several minutes ago."

Avery considered throwing the glass at him, then changed her mind and drank the awful mixture. She shuddered again and handed the glass to him.

"I'm thirty-three, Jerkins. Thirty-three." She fell back onto the pillow with a moan and stared dolefully at the ceiling. "Three decades and three years."

She shuddered and felt like crying.

"It's a good age," Jerkins suggested.

"Nonsense, Jerkins. Thirty-three is only a good age if you're married and have five children. Otherwise, you're regarded by all and sundry as an ancient curiosity much like a mummy in the exhibit in the Egyptian Hall in Piccadilly."

"I happen to like mummies, my lady. They are quite fascinating."

"How old are you, Jerkins?"

"I am forty-three."

"Goodness! Really? Come to think of it, for you that is quite young. I'd have thought you were much older. Fifty or sixty at the most." She looked at him thought-fully. The truth was that Jerkins could be any age from thirty upwards. He wore a bag wig made of horsehair with grey curls at the sides and back, spectacles, and livery consisting of black breeches, a long old-fashioned blue coat trimmed in gold, and a beige waistcoat. The clothes hung loosely on his tall, lanky frame. He hunched his shoulders and squinted through his glasses, which made him appear almost elderly. But his face was unlined, his nose eagle-like and proud, and his eyes... Well. She'd already spent far too much time admiring his eyes.

She handed him the glass.

"Thank you, my lady. Now, may I suggest you rise

and have some breakfast. After that, we shall have to talk."

"Talk? About what? My head still hurts, I am still tired, and I want to sleep. Besides, it's only morning." She yawned.

"It's nearly three in the afternoon, my lady."

Avery shot up. "What?"

"You've been asleep all day."

"Impossible." She looked at the window again. It was true. Her room faced west, so the sun only shone into her room in the afternoon.

She scrambled out of bed. She was still wearing her dress from the previous day, now hopelessly wrinkled, and her boots were by the bed. Jerkins must have taken them off.

She swallowed. "I'll meet you in the dining room for breakfast."

"Very good, my lady."

JERKINS WAS RIGHT. A solid breakfast and good, strong coffee revived her spirits. The headache had subsided, but the gloomy feeling of depression still hovered over her like a black storm cloud. She attempted to chase it away.

"Well, Jerkins. What did you want to talk to me about?" Avery tried to catch a glimpse of his grey eyes, but all she could see was the sunlight glinting off the frames of his glasses.

"I wanted to respectfully enquire, my lady, when you intend to resume your journey to Dorset."

She folded her napkin into a triangle, and then into a smaller and smaller one, until it was so tiny she could no longer fold it. Then she let go, and the whole napkin unfolded with a bounce. It was strangely satisfying. She repeated the action.

"I'm not going."

"I see."

"At least not today. It's my birthday, and I don't want to spend it in a coach."

"That's perfectly understandable, my lady."

"Yes." She tugged at her lower lip. "In fact, I was thinking of spending several days here. It's not like you must pack up the house right away, is it? No one will miss these things now that my brother is on his way to the Continent." She waved her arm around. "So, it won't matter if everything is packed a week earlier or later."

A pause. "I suppose not, my lady."

"In fact, come to think of it, no one will notice if it is packed up a month from now. Or maybe even two." Or three. Or four.

Or half a year.

Jerkins cleared his throat. "Your ladyship intends to stay here, then?"

"For the time being, yes. Unless the landlord needs the house, of course." That would ruin everything, and she would have to leave immediately.

"He's out of the country at the moment and not expected back any time soon," Jerkins put in.

Suddenly Avery's spirits rose. "How very obliging of him. Well, Jerkins, the thing is, my brother clearly has no use for the house, and neither does the landlord. And I would very much like to stay. Do you understand? No one will ever know if I stay a little longer." Except for Great-Aunt Euphemia, but she could always write her a letter to tell her of her change of plans, and she would have to invent a little fib. "That is, provided you don't inform the landlord. Or my brother," she added after a pause.

Jerkins looked back at her with his impassive face. "I wouldn't tell either of them."

Avery exhaled. "Excellent. So that's the plan: I shall stay for the entire Season."

That seemed to rattle him. "The entire Season?"

"Yes."

"All on your own? Without so much as a companion?"

"Why not?"

Never mind that it was highly unorthodox, if not improper, for a lady to stay in her brother's townhouse during the Season, entirely alone.

"I've never had a Season. One would think it would be high time to remedy that." She lifted her chin.

"I... see." He blinked at her, then caught himself. "In that case, my lady, I'll have to recall some of the other retainers."

She shook her head. "No. I don't want anyone." The thought of being completely alone in the house, free to do as she pleased, elated her so much it took her breath away. Why bring back the whole train of servants? "Actually, Jerkins, I think it would be best if you left for Penmaron Hall as well. I shall be quite fine on my own, here."

"I don't think that's possible, my lady," Jerkins replied

gently. "If my services are required here, then of course I shall stay."

"But I don't want you here."

He deliberately ignored her. "You will also need a lady's maid, a cook, a footman, and a housekeeper. In addition to a companion, of course."

"I won't need any of them." Her head began to throb again.

Jerkins's eyebrows almost disappeared in his hairline. "But my lady, you cannot possibly stay here alone without a companion. It would be highly unorthodox."

"Unorthodox." Avery pulled on her lower lips. "Heaven forbid an unmarried woman like myself stay alone in her brother's townhouse, with only the butler around." She threw him an arch look. "How excessively improper! What would people say?"

Jerkins shifted from one foot to another, and she watched with interest how a dull red crept up his neck. "Indeed, my lady. There will be talk. It would not do at all."

"Nonsense, Jerkins. You forget that spinsters are invisible. No one will be interested in what Lady Avery Heywood, ape leader, is up to. I have no reputation to lose. Besides, I'll do very well looking after myself." She'd have freedom. Complete freedom. No unruly children to look after, no testy brothers to tiptoe around, no capricious sisters-in-law to placate, no patronising housekeepers to instruct, no servants to direct, no pernickety butlers to deal with.

She could sleep however long she wanted; she could walk around barefoot in her nightdress all day without risking a raised eyebrow from the butler. She could lie on the sofa in the study and read all day. She could work through her Never List, item by item, without worrying about what the servants thought of her. It would be perfect. Her spirits soared. And she would have no companions, footmen, or butlers traipsing after her, telling her what to do.

As if to prove her point, Jerkins followed her doggedly as she made her way to the study.

It did not escape her notice that the desk was now tidy, the quills sorted, the papers stacked to the side. She was relieved to see her list on top of the pile.

Hopefully Jerkins hadn't read it. How embarrassing if he had.

She'd already crossed off two points, namely smoking a cigar and drinking whisky. She stared at the third point and wondered if she'd been entirely out of her mind when she'd written this: shoot a gun. What on earth?

"Pardon the interruption, but has her ladyship ever emptied the slops?"

"I beg your pardon?" Avery looked up from the paper.

Jerkins, the accursed creature, was still there, hands clasped behind his back, lips pursed, waiting for an answer. "This question relates to our earlier conversation, in which her ladyship insisted on staying for the entire duration of the Season in this house and that retainers would not be required. In practical terms, that would mean that her ladyship would have to fetch her own coal, light her own fire, clean her own shoes and clothes, purchase victuals at the various markets and prepare her own meals, and, lastly, to empty her own chamber pot." He ticked off each item with his gloved fingers.

She opened her mouth. She closed it with a snap. She swallowed.

"No," she finally admitted. "I've never emptied the slops."

"I thought so." Jerkins looked satisfied. "That's why her ladyship will need a housemaid."

Blast it, but he was right. Unless she had a house-maid, she would have to learn how to remove her own slops. She had no idea how to go about doing so. Bury it in the garden? Hurl it into the street? Hardly. And how did one go about preparing a meal? She may be the spin-ster of the household, but she was an earl's daughter and had never cleared the grate, let alone fetched coal from the coal hole.

"We most certainly need someone to cook," Jerkins added.

"We?" Avery drew out the word.

"We. For my own cooking skills do not extend beyond toast, egg, coffee, and kidneys, my lady."

"You cooked that?" Of course he had, if the cook was no longer here. "It was delicious, Jerkins."

"Thank you, my lady. The point is, if her ladyship intends to stay for the Season, we shall have to hire domestic servants, for the others are required at Penmaron Hall."

She had to admit that Jerkins was right. She needed an abigail to help her dress and a footman to run errands. She also needed someone to do the cooking. It was almost a whole household.

But there was one problem.

"I can't possibly afford to pay you all full wages." Avery lifted her shoulders. "Not for a whole Season." She had some savings, but they were intended for the time after Great-Aunt Euphemia. It looked as if she would have to use it before then, for Seasons were said to be exorbitantly expensive.

"Now that Lord Fothergill is travelling, we're on board wages, my lady, if that's relevant." This meant that servants received an allowance for board and lodging while their employer was away.

"But board wages are not full wages, and you would have to work for me full time," Avery argued. "That would hardly be fair."

She pulled at her lower lip as she thought. Then she unclasped the emerald bracelet she wore around her wrist. It had been her mother's, a family heirloom which she'd treasured. Selena had glanced at it more than once with a covetous expression on her face.

After a moment's hesitation, Avery handed it to Jerkins. "Take this and pawn it and use it to pay the servants and anything else needed for the household. It should last us through the Season."

There it was again.

That strange flicker in his eyes.

After some hesitation, Jerkins took the bracelet.

"Very well, my lady. I will see what can be done."

Chapter Four

Now that Jerkins had finally left, she could get down to what really mattered.

Point Three: Shooting a Pistol.

Finding one in this household wasn't a problem, as her brother was an obsessive collector of duelling pistols, especially if they had belonged to famous people in the past. Avery went to the cabinet in the corner where Tom kept his precious collection.

He had boasted that he owned a pair that had belonged to Louis XIV. It must be the two elaborately engraved pistols overlaid with gold that were the centre-piece of the cabinet. Avery knew nothing about them, but even she could see they looked too beautiful and extrava-gant to be useful. Then there was Oliver Cromwell's pistol, or so Tom claimed. It looked old and rusty. In the end, there was no proof it had ever belonged to Cromwell.

The *pièce de résistance*, and what Avery was really after, was the plain, dark brown flintlock that looked like it had been heavily used. Tom claimed it had belonged to Jax Tyrrell, the legendary highwayman. It was with this weapon that he'd supposedly held up his unfortunate victims on Hounslow Heath. That was before he had been caught and hanged.

Avery turned it in her hands and peered at it. The steel fitting was monogrammed JT.

She picked up the powder horn that lay beside it and marched into the narrow garden dotted with enough trees and shrubs to give her privacy.

In the middle of the back yard stood a cherry tree.

That would be her target.

She would take a practice aim with an empty barrel and then see if she could manage to load the gun for the real shot.

She closed one eye, squinted at the tree with the other, took aim and pulled the trigger.

The blast sent her staggering backwards.

Avery dropped the weapon.

Jerkins came running. "Are you hurt?" He grabbed her shoulders.

"It was loaded!" she gasped. "Tom must be out of his mind to have a loaded pistol lying around the house."

Jerkins towered over her with a scowl. "You weren't trying to shoot yourself, were you?"

"Nonsense, Jerkins. What makes you think that? I was trying to shoot the tree."

But Jerkins was still hovering over her with a worried frown.

"You can let me go now; I am perfectly all right. But

apparently the tree isn't. See?" Avery walked over to the tree and ran her fingers along the bark. "It's a hit!"

"A stroke of luck, my lady."

"Poppycock, Jerkins. I seem to have the hidden talents of a markswoman." She picked up the pistol and handed it happily to him. "Reload it, please."

Jerkins held the weapon between two fingers and looked at it distastefully. "I emphatically disapprove of weapons of violence."

"So do I. But this is an experiment. You know how to load a gun, do you not?"

Jerkins puckered up. "My lady. I am a butler. I am not in the habit of loading guns."

"You have to put the powder in the muzzle, followed by a wad of cloth and the lead ball. Mind you, first the cloth, then the ball, not the other way round," Avery lectured. "Use the ramrod to stuff it all down. This much I do know, because I saw my father and brother do it countless times when they went hunting. It isn't all that difficult."

Jerkins grumbled but did as he was told. Then he handed it to her.

"Can you see Jax Tyrrell using this to hold up his victims? I have to say, I don't really think it was his, even though his initials are engraved on it." She brought it closer to her eyes, pointing the muzzle directly at Jerkins, who froze. "It's definitely a J and a T."

"My lady—"

"But who knows, it could very well be Jake Thorne or John Taylor or Jim Thompson. There must be a large number of men with those initials." She waved the gun in front of his face. "Jonathan Tully."

"Please, my lady..."

"You know what I think, Jerkins? I think it would have been very careless of a highwayman to engrave his name on his weapon of crime. If that pistol really belonged to Jax Tyrrell, he couldn't have been very bright, so perhaps it served him right that he was caught and hanged in the end."

With that she turned, closed one eye, aimed at the tree, and fired.

Jerkins flinched and clapped his hands over his ears.

"It's another hit! What did I tell you? I'm a brilliant shot." Avery handed the pistol to Jerkins, pulled out her sheet of paper and pencil, and crossed out point three with a flourish.

"It's quite satisfying to know I might have the makings of a highwaywoman." Avery nodded to herself.

Jerkins merely replied with a choke.

"Mind you, not that I would ever want to be a highway robber like Moll Cutpurse, who was very wicked and very scandalous. I firmly believe that highway robbery is vile. It only sounds nice in legends and in the stories I tell the boys. But it is somewhat satisfying to know I might have some unexpected talents other than..." *Being a spinster*, she was about to say, but she stopped and swallowed her words.

"If I may express my humble opinion, my lady," Jerkins interjected timidly.

"You may."

"If I might be so bold as to suggest, rather than going

about shooting, erm, hapless cherry trees, if you are looking for a more productive occupation in which you might put your talents to use, and which, to boot, might bring in some financial income as well, why not write down all the wonderful stories you have told your nephews and see whether they can be published? Under a male pseudonym, of course," he added hastily.

Avery stared at him. "Are you out of your mind, Jerkins?"

He shrugged. "Well, it is commonly known that story papers like *The Young Gentleman's Magazine* publish mystery, adventure, and crime stories, and I happen to know they are always on the lookout for talented new writers."

"But most of those stories are awful and badly written."

"Exactly, my lady, which brings me to my point. The stories you have invented are of a higher quality than what is currently being printed there."

She stared at him. "You have been eavesdropping on our nightly story time?"

"Oh no, my lady, I would never presume to do so." His smoky grey eyes were wide with innocence.

"Jerkins."

"Perhaps once or twice."

"Jerkins!"

"It was only a suggestion, but I can see it is a bad idea, so pray forget I mentioned it. I will go now and lock up the pistols." He walked away, holding the offending item in front of him, muttering, "And lose the key."

Avery stared after him. That Jerkins! Always so unassuming and proper, and then he came up with ideas like this. It was fantastic, of course—improper, and utterly undoable. She was an earl's daughter, not a writer of sensational stories.

She could never do that.

What a preposterous idea to write down those silly stories she'd loved to tell her nephews about highwaymen, pirates, vampires, ghosts, and ghouls. And under a male pseudonym? Tosh and nonsense.

She shook her head, then stared at her Never List.

With her tongue poking out of one corner of her mouth, she scribbled: "Write and publish stories and become decadently famous," at the bottom of her list.

Chapter Five

After a light luncheon consisting of a small shepherd's pie, which the cook had left for Jerkins in the pantry and some tea, Avery was back in her brother's study, head in hands, poring over her precious Never List:

Point 4: *Have a Season.*

She sighed.

Having a Season was as impossible as sailing with Captain James Cook on the *Endeavour* to the Antipodes. She could wish for it with all her might, dream about it, map it out in her imagination, but it would always remain an impossibility.

Her father had died before he was able to launch her into society; then her mother had been ill. By then, she'd been far too old for a Season.

But a Season she wanted, and a Season she would have. It was point four on her list, after all.

She had no idea how to go about accomplishing this on her own. One needed sponsors and connections, invitations, and even more connections, for one did not simply take part in the *ton*'s events. One had to be accepted and approved by the *haut ton*.

Sailing to the Antipodes might be easier to accomplish, Avery feared.

Having a Season meant spending a fortune on a new wardrobe, being introduced at court, receiving and being received by the Quality. It meant parties and balls, theatres and operas, picnics and ridottos, riding on Rotten Row, walking in the parks and much more. All for the express purpose of finding a husband.

Is that what it was all about? A desire to marry? Avery pinched her lower lip so hard it hurt.

Tosh and nonsense. Of course not.

Of course, yes!

She didn't want a husband.

Certainly, she wanted one!

But... that wasn't entirely true, either.

What point was there to have a husband like Tom, who spent the entire day at the club, only to return in the evening to change his clothes and then leave again to go to some political dinner without his wife? They barely saw each other and lived separate lives in the same house, like strangers. The connecting door between them always remained firmly locked, the servants had whispered.

If all husbands were like that, she could do without one, thank you very much.

But the thought of a male companion at her side, who understood her, who shared her interests, who read books with her by the fireplace, who told her amusing stories and made her laugh, was so lovely that it hurt.

She didn't want to hunt for one. She would rather die than wheedle a man into overlooking her pale visage and flat chest and marry her just because she was an earl's daughter. She supposed that her connection to her brother, the current Earl of Fothergill, might mean something to fortune hunters, but as soon as they found out her father had gambled away her dowry long ago and that she had only a small allowance, they would probably drop her.

Not that anyone would ever be slightly interested in her to begin with, once they saw she was a thirty-three-year-old ape leader. Fact was, she was far too old to get married.

She sighed.

But still. She'd promised herself a Season.

How?

Avery leaned back in her chair; her forehead puckered to a frown.

Her brother hadn't given a tuppence about the Season; it had been Selena who'd been the socialite. Selena, who'd sent out invitations and who'd received invitations. They'd come in daily, keeping Jerkins quite busy sorting them.

Avery jumped up and went into Selena's morning room. Her writing desk was strewn with scraps of paper, cards, quills, powder, ribbons, a pot of rouge, hairpins, a hairbrush with blonde strands of hair in it, and an empty flask of perfume that smelled like Selena—simultaneously cloying and acrid.

She picked up a pile of letters and sifted through them. They were invitations Selena had tossed aside. Most of them were for events in the past, but oh! Here was one. Avery pulled it out. A ticket to a public charity ball tomorrow night.

She tapped the card against her lips. This would be very good. All she needed now was a dress... and a companion.

Finding a suitable dress was not an issue. Avery looked at the pile of discarded dresses Selena had left on the bed. She was surprised Mrs Billings hadn't kept them herself or distributed them among the female servants. Whatever the reason, they were still here, and they would be of use to Avery now.

She lifted a lemon-yellow sarsenet dress from the pile and held it to her front, admiring herself in the mirror. It had a net of a similar colour over it, with a small train. One thing could be said about Selena: she certainly had taste. Avery was about the same height as her sister-in-law but had a much smaller bust. It would be rather loose at the top, unless she took it in. Jerkins had said he'd hire a lady's maid for her, but by then the ball would be long over. She'd have to hem in the superfluous fabric herself to tighten the dress on the top. Otherwise, the gown was quite lovely, and the silk flowed nicely.

On to the bigger problem: the escort. Where to get one? Normally, fathers, brothers, cousins, or other relatives accompanied ladies to balls, and in the absence of these, a widowed or married chaperone. But Avery was well past the age when she was expected to have a chaperone; her brother was abroad, and she was not on speaking terms with any of her male relatives who weren't as old as Methuselah. The few women in her family who were married had long since died.

"What to do?" Avery mused aloud. She could hardly go to the ball alone, could she? She imagined arriving at the door of the great house, handing her invitation to a haughty-looking doorkeeper whose eyes would sweep over her shoulders looking for her escort and, finding none, deny her entry.

Perhaps she could pretend her escort had already entered the ball.

Assuming that worked, what would she do once inside?

Avery might have never been to a ball, but she was not naive enough to think she would be accepted by society without proper connections.

After some thought, she pulled the bell.

Jerkins appeared promptly.

"I have somewhat of a conundrum." Avery handed him the invitation.

Jerkins took it with gloved fingers and perused it. Both his eyebrows rose. "I apprehend the gist of the matter, my lady."

"Do you, indeed? That is most impressive."

"Indeed. It would be my pleasure to offer a solution."

"The ball is tomorrow. What sort of solution do you have in mind?"

Jerkins made a mysterious face. "I have my means. Your ladyship need not concern herself with such details." He produced a pocket watch. "The new abigail, Emma, is due to arrive today, just in time to help with the wardrobe."

"How very efficient of you, Jerkins."

"One attempts to do one's best, my lady."

"Oh. Jerkins?"

He paused at the door. "My lady?"

"Could you please stop that?"

He blinked. "'Pardon, my lady?"

"This. This, *my ladying*. Now that it's just you and me in the house, and, well, later the maid and some other staff, you don't have to say 'my lady' in every sentence, at least when no one else is around. Makes me feel positively ancient."

"Certainly, my lady. Which reminds me that my lady might reconsider the issue of having a companion in the house—"

"Jerkins!"

He bowed and left, but not before Avery had detected a faint smirk on his face.

Chapter Six

THE NEXT MORNING, TO AVERY'S SURPRISE, SHE received her first morning caller. This was unusual due to two reasons: firstly, she had never received a caller before (something else to add and scratch off her Never List), at least no one who'd wanted to see her and not her brother or sister-in-law. And secondly, the morning caller had arrived in the morning, just as Avery was eating her breakfast, and not in the early afternoon, as was customary.

She dropped the silver spoon into her porridge bowl with a clatter as Jerkins, pompous as ever, announced, "Mrs Wimplethorpe is here to see you, my lady." He presented her card on a small silver tray.

Avery picked it up. "Mrs Belinda Wimplethorpe." She turned the card over, but there wasn't much more on it than that name in elaborate gold cursive. "Well. That's not very informative. Who could this be?"

She crumpled her napkin, dropped it on the table, and rose to go into the drawing room.

A slender woman stood by the window, her back to Avery.

Avery had never seen a woman so garishly dressed. She was wearing a saffron-coloured walking dress with dark blue frogging criss-crossing the front, and tassels. Lots of them. The collar, hem, and sleeves were trimmed with brown mink. A red-turquoise Kashmir shawl hung loosely around her shoulders. On her ginger head she wore a moss-green turban decorated with ribbons, lace, and flowers. The entire ensemble was wildly colourful, but oddly enough, it looked elegant and, Avery thought, expensive.

The moment Avery entered, the woman turned and paused, sizing her up with one glance. Then her face broke into a broad smile. She opened her arms wide. "Cousin!"

Cousin?

Mrs Wimplethorpe stepped gingerly towards her and kissed both her cheeks. Or rather, she kissed the air above her cheeks two, three times.

Avery found herself enveloped in a cloud of roses and lilies of the valley.

"What a pleasure it is to meet you at last," Mrs Wimplethorpe gushed.

"Erm, yes. Likewise." Avery blinked at her. "Forgive me, but how exactly are we acquainted?" she asked after motioning for her to sit.

"Oh! It is a bit around several corners, for our family is so extensive, is it not? Uncle Hubert, you know?"

Avery frowned. "I'm not certain."

"Aunt Frederica's husband?"

"Aunt Frederica...oh! You mean the one who—"

"...went to Italy and then stayed there." Mrs Wimplethorpe leaned forward, and her eyes sparkled as she said, "The truth is that she eloped with her lover, but Uncle Hubert wanted us all to know that she travelled there on account of the good climate and her ailing health."

"Oh! I honestly can't recall..."

Mrs Wimplethorpe waved a narrow, gloved hand. "It matters not, since all this happened long before the French wars. Every family has a secret hidden in the attic. This happens to be ours. Anyhow, where was I? Uncle Hubert. Well, our Uncle Hubert had a brother, the third, whose wife's cousin is my sister."

Avery's head spun as she attempted to reconstruct the family relationship. Finally, she gave up and smiled weakly at Mrs Wimplethorpe. "Cousins, then."

"As I said. Cousins." She beamed at Avery.

"Now, Mrs Wimplethorpe—"

"Belinda. You must call me Belinda, and I'll call you Avery, yes?"

"Well, Belinda—"

"I am here, of course, because I heard you were in town and since you are living here all on your own, in need of a companion. I am happy to move in for the duration of your stay here to provide companionship." She smiled beatifically.

"Oh. Oh!" Now Avery understood. Mrs Belinda Wimplethorpe wasn't her real cousin at all. She must be the 'solution' Jerkins had promised her the day before. Who was she really? An actress? Was she really married?

And where had he found her so quickly? And what on earth was Jerkins thinking, having a stranger move in with her?

Avery sat up straight. "Thank you for your concern, but that really is not necessary."

Belinda's lips formed to a round, red O. "But Cousin, you can't possibly stay here all on your own. What will people think?"

"Mrs Wimplethorpe—"

"Belinda, please."

She sighed. "Belinda. Cousin. It matters not what people think. No one knows me, and no one cares that I'm here."

"But Cousin, this simply won't do. You are here to experience the Season, are you not? Well, even if you do not care to have a companion stay with you at the house—and I strongly encourage you to change your mind on this issue, for sooner or later people will discover you are living here alone, and this would not be at all good for one's reputation—you will need an escort, nonetheless. Think of all the balls! You cannot possibly go to a ball on your own. In fact, there is one this very evening. I would very much like to accompany you to the charity ball tonight. I hear it will be such a squeeze, and I simply adore squeezes."

"How did you know I was thinking of going to the charity ball?"

Belinda looked at her wide-eyed. "But naturally you would want to go! It will be all the crack." Belinda chattered on and on about the ball, and how lovely it would certainly be. "I hear it's going to be all Mediterranean style. It will make you long to see Italy for yourself. I have yet to visit Venice."

Jerkins entered, bringing a tray of tea and scones. Avery gave him a piercing look, but his face was as inscrutable as ever. She poured the tea, wondering whether she could trust Belinda Wimplethorpe.

Belinda sipped her heavily sugared tea, her little finger jutting into the air as she held the delicate porcelain cup.

Was this really a good solution? Dare she continue? Would Belinda Wimplethorpe, whoever she really was, be a good companion at her first London ball? But if not her, then who?

"What do you say, Avery? Shall we set out and conquer the beau monde? My connections are excellent, you see. I daresay we will enjoy ourselves tremendously tonight. And who knows, after tonight you might accept me as a companion for your home as well. You might find me an unobtrusive companion who mostly sleeps during the day. I have insomnia, you see, and I simply cannot sleep a wink at night. Nights are for balls and parties, wouldn't you agree?"

There was a mischievous twinkle in her dark eyes.

Avery decided she liked her.

She was a colourful bundle of energy with a sense of humour.

Never mind that they weren't really related. For tonight, she would pretend to be her cousin.

Avery raised her teacup in greeting. "I will think about it. In the meantime, conquer the beau monde we shall."

Chapter Seven

AVERY'S FIRST BALL WASN'T AT ALL WHAT SHE'D expected. The entire ballroom sparkled with lights reflecting off the crystal chandeliers. Orange and lemon blossoms, palm trees, and wreaths of ivy adorned the room. It was all lovely but overdone, bordering on the excessive. The ball was far grander than she'd imagined— and more crowded than the Bartholomew Fair. The musicians, seated on a platform, fiddled enthusiastically, and there was a general din of chatter and bursts of laughter over the strains of music. The air was stale with sweat, perfume, and alcohol. Small clusters of people stood at the sides sipping champagne handed out by liveried footmen, and ladies rested on chairs and sofas along the walls, observing and commenting on the activity around them.

It was both glamorous and overwhelming, exhilarating and terrifying.

Avery paused at the door to watch the groups of well-dressed dancers take their places on the floor for a quadrille. Ah, she knew these steps! She'd practised them with the boys until they'd all dropped in exhaustion. Since she had four nephews, she'd had to stand in when they rehearsed, so she'd had more than enough practice in all manner of country dances, quadrilles, the cotillion, and even the waltz. Her foot tapped in rhythm with the music.

She was so engrossed in watching the couples dance that she lost sight of Belinda Wimplethorpe, who'd entered the room a few steps ahead of her and immediately disappeared into the crowd.

It was too late for Avery to panic that she was standing alone in a ballroom full of strangers. Apart from Belinda, who was now firmly swallowed up in the whale's stomach of a ballroom, she didn't know a single soul.

On her right was a group of fashionable ladies and gentlemen discussing the premiere of Rossini's latest opera. On her left, a group of ladies gossiped about the latest fashions. They were all wearing ball gowns with low necklines, gauze over satin slips, exquisitely decorated with flounces, lace, and flowers. Their gowns were cut above the ankle.

Avery realised immediately that her own dress was outdated. Why hadn't she thought of it before? Of course Selena would only give away dresses that were out of fashion. Her dress had the simple, vertical, turn-of-the-century silhouette, with no embellishments, trimmings, or flounces, and was long enough to drape across the floor. It was a nuisance because Avery had stepped on her own hem more than once.

To confirm this, one of the fashionable ladies looked

her up and down, pausing at the trodden hem and raising a fine eyebrow at her high-cut neckline. Having decided she was no longer worthy of further scrutiny, she turned her back.

"Do you know her?" asked a lady in a purple turban standing next to her.

"No. A dowdy old tabby. It is well known that at these public balls they allow all and sundry to enter as long as they have a ticket. *Entre nous*, I find it most tedious and much prefer the more exclusive balls at Almack's where the patronesses would never grant entry to the likes of her." The woman's voice carried to her in crisp, clear tones.

A hot wave of shame flushed over Avery's body. The words smarted as painfully as if she'd fallen naked into a cluster of burning nettles.

Blistering with humiliation, she elbowed her way through the crowd, only to bump into a couple attempting a twirl. She stumbled into the middle of a group of dancers, breaking up the formation. The group of fashionable, haughty ladies tittered.

Fie! She behaved worse than a drunken country bumpkin who'd never set foot in a ballroom before. Well, at least the last part of that statement was true.

Avery dropped into a chair against the wall, exhausted. She put her hands to her burning cheeks.

Where was Belinda?

And why hadn't she told her that her dress was unfashionable?

The truth was that Belinda hadn't seen her dress until they'd arrived here, because Avery had been wearing her cloak, and they'd both been far too distracted to study each other's dresses when they'd arrived at the ball.

Disconcerted, she realised she barely knew what dress Belinda was wearing. Had it been moss green? She barely remembered. But there was no moss green anywhere in the crowd.

Avery wrung her hands and tried to calm herself. One dance passed, then a second. She'd spent an entire hour sitting.

She would have danced, gladly, if someone had asked her, but no one had.

And who would ever ask, since it was highly unlikely that a gentleman would ask a lady to dance with him if they had not been introduced?

She could have kicked herself. How could she have disregarded such a basic rule of etiquette? It was so rigid, so inflexible, as if set in stone: "Thou shalt not dance unless thou hath first been introduced." It could be extended to: "Thou shalt not speak to anyone unless thou hath been introduced."

But who would introduce her, and to whom?

It would have been Belinda's role to do so, but Avery had begun to doubt whether she was truly up to the task. Certainly not, if she was just an actress hired by Jerkins.

So here she was, sitting against the wall, completely invisible, as if she were part of the wallpaper pattern.

No one acknowledged her presence. It was as if there were an invisible bubble around her, preventing people from getting too close. The only woman who had noticed her had snubbed and insulted her.

Bile rose in her throat, and she blinked back a hot rush of tears.

This was not how she'd imagined her first ball.

When the waltz started, her favourite of all dances, Avery could stand it no longer. She jumped to her feet and made her way back across the room, back to the foyer.

A footman was standing by the entrance, holding a tray of drinks. She grabbed one and drank the whole glass of champagne. As she replaced the glass, she asked, "Where would I find the ladies' retirement room?"

"Down the hall, third door on the left, my lady," the footman replied.

Avery gave him a smile. Brilliant fellow! If she could, she'd pat herself on the back for having exchanged a few words with someone other than Belinda. One could consider that a progress, even if he was a footman.

A group of ladies emerged from the retirement room, and when she went in, she found herself alone, save for a maidservant.

She stepped up to a full-length mirror and studied her appearance.

She didn't think she looked all that bad. Jerkins had certainly seemed to think she looked lovely. Not that he'd actually said so, but it had been in those expressive eyes of his, which had rested on her with an intent gaze that had made her feel rather warm and tingly.

Her new abigail had arranged her white-blonde hair in a pretty coiffure that set off her swan-like neck and slender figure.

She lifted the yellow cloth and pointed her toes

encased in satin slippers. She was proud of her ankles. They were trim and shapely and worth showing off.

"I must say, you're not quite a hag yet." She pulled back the skin around her eyes, which had developed some distinct laugh lines. She liked those lines; they expressed character.

"And as far as I can tell, you're neither deaf nor blind, and all your teeth are still intact." She bared two rows of pearly white teeth. "And not to forget, you're healthier than a horse, so no matter what they say, these are all things to be thankful for, even if they like to impress upon you at every turn that you're a dotty old maid in her dotage—"

A muffled snort of laughter filled the room.

Avery whirled round.

A lady stepped out from behind a Chinese-lacquered screen in the corner, where she must have been all the time, overhearing her soliloquy.

She was one of the most glamorous creatures Avery had ever seen. She wore a midnight-blue gown, cinched under her bosom with an ornate gold and emerald belt. Matching earrings dangled from her ears, so long they almost touched her creamy bare shoulders. Her curly black hair cascaded around a pointed face, and her expressive dark eyes twinkled with humour. She wore a burgundy velvet turban that sat rakishly on her baby curls. In her hand she clutched a fistful of her gown, which was trimmed with feathers. She looked more magnificent than the Queen herself.

Well, wonderful. Now Avery had humiliated herself in front of royalty, or worse.

"I beg your pardon," she stammered. "I thought I was alone." She wondered if she ought to be curtsying.

"No, no, no! Pray, no apologies, for the fault is mine entirely, ensconcing myself behind this screen. I have been struggling with my dress, which has been vexing me, and I have sent my abigail away to fetch a new one; but she is taking far too long. The ball will be over before she returns, and I must make a mental note to bring at least two dresses to future balls to avoid eventualities like this. I can't possibly let myself be seen in public like this."

"But you're beautiful!" Avery blurted out.

The lady beamed at her. "Do you think so?" Then her face fell. "But look at this. Pray, tell me. What do you say to this horror?" She lifted her dress. "Do you like this?"

Avery wrinkled her nose as she studied it.

"Pray, be honest. I must hear the truth, however painful."

"Honestly? No."

The woman sighed dramatically, as if she'd pronounced a death sentence. "I knew it!"

"This embellishment seems somewhat superfluous, as your dress is breathtaking on its own. But then, you'd probably look magnificent in a turnip sack."

The lady gave her an astonished look, then burst into a high, tinkling laugh. "I like you. You are so refreshing. It's the feather, isn't it?" She lifted the dress, which had an enormous, long white feather sewn into it.

"Makes you look a bit like a squirrel with a long white fluffy tail." Realising what she'd just said, Avery clamped both hands over her mouth.

"A squirrel!" The lady groaned.

"I do beg your pardon! That was horribly rude. I should have said a peacock dragging its tail behind it."

"Worse and worse! No, don't amend your initial assessment of me. It is an accurate one. I did ask you to be honest." She shook her dress and pursed her lips in a discontented moue. "What on earth am I supposed to do about it?"

Avery regarded her for one moment. Then she stepped up to the lady. "May I?"

"Please!"

Avery knelt behind her and immediately saw what the problem was. The feather, an overgrown, fluffy white thing, was sweeping the floor behind her like a dusting mop, no doubt causing all and sundry to step on it, including the lady herself. It was sewn with light stitches to a train. How one could dance or sit with such a thing attached to one's derriere was a mystery; it must be one of those illogical things the ladies of the beau monde do in the name of fashion.

As if reading her mind, the lady said, "I had asked my modiste to make a unique creation that would start a new fashion trend. I wanted something different, something truly memorable, something divine, and she insisted this would become all the crack. However, I was never really convinced. Trains have been quite out of date for years, unless one is presented at court. How tedious it is!"

"Hm." Avery tugged on the feather, which was only lightly stitched to the fabric. Without much ado, Avery pulled it off with a rip. She held the feather up to the lady, who looked down at her in astonishment.

"There it is: the offending appendage. On its own, it

is rather beautiful. A shame not to use it, however. You could drape it around your shoulders; it is long enough. Or attach it to your headwear?" Avery lifted it to the velvet creation she wore on her head and draped the feather forward so that it hung over one shoulder.

The lady stared into the mirror with round eyes. "Goodness me!" Then she turned to Avery. "This is ingenious!" She clapped her hands. "Yes! This is it!"

"If you want, I can sew it on for you," Avery offered.

"Oh, could you? I confess I'm terrible with a needle myself, and Fanny shows no sign of returning."

Avery motioned for the maidservant to provide her with needle and thread and asked the lady to sit in a chair while she sewed.

"Now, tell me all about what you were talking about earlier," the lady said. "The part about you being in your dotage."

Avery blushed. "It was nothing. I was merely feeling sorry for myself."

"It's not nothing. There is a story behind it. I love stories. Tell me," the lady commanded. It was clear she would not tolerate any contradiction.

So, before she knew it, Avery was blurting out all her troubles, starting with her thirty-third birthday, this being her first ball, how she'd lost her cousin Belinda, and how disastrous it had all been so far.

"The truth is that I've been firmly on the shelf since I was sixteen, and society cast me early into the role of a ridiculous old ape leader. I am afraid I will start to act like one, you know. To really become one of those sad, lonely, silly, doddering old maids they like to portray in those satirical prints. I have no sense of fashion at all and no idea how to behave in society. So maybe what they say is true. And now I can't believe I've just poured all this nonsense into your ears, so please forget what I've said. I am indeed turning into a chatty old woman, spewing forth nothing but a farrago of nonsense." Avery sighed.

"Oh, fie! You're only as old as you feel inside. Me, I feel sixteen forever inside, can you tell? Upon my word, I am normally all for rules and etiquette, especially when it comes to navigating the social scene, but never allow society to dictate who you are. You are a strong woman, and I like strong women. You have the makings of an eccentric, and that is a breed of woman who is not only strong, but independent and, while no one likes to admit it, secretly admired, if not feared, because they have managed to rise above the strictures of society."

Avery was genuinely touched. "Thank you. That is the nicest thing anyone has ever said to me."

"About your appearance. Come here."

Avery cut the thread with the scissors and stepped in front of her.

The woman eyed her critically. "Aside from the cut of your dress, which is fine but outdated, the problem is the colour. That citrus yellow doesn't suit your complexion at all; it makes you look washed out. You have such pale skin that you need to wear a stronger, more vibrant colour. Cobalt blue, emerald green—especially emerald green—would look lovely on you and bring out the colour of your eyes. Maybe even a strong red."

"I've always wanted a red dress," Avery said wistfully.

"Then you must wear red. It will suit you to perfection. Pluck your eyebrows and darken them slightly. It is a trick I use, and it brings out the eyes."

"Cosmetics? Isn't that frowned upon?" The natural, clean-scrubbed look on women was currently en vogue.

The lady smiled. "Only if it is obvious you are actually using them. The trick is to apply the paint in such a manner that no one can tell you are wearing it."

The lady stood and admired her newly adorned headdress in the mirror. "I am truly pleased." She held out her hand. "Do call me Sally. I'm truly in your debt, Miss...?"

"Lady Avery Heywood." Avery touched her slender gloved fingers, but the lady took her hand in a firm clasp and held it.

"Heywood," the woman mused. "Are you perchance related to the Earl of Fothergill?"

"My brother."

"Ah. A brilliant diplomat, or so they say. We hear he has been sent to Vienna on a diplomatic mission."

"Yes, he and his family left yesterday."

"He cuts a good figure but never dances, whereas Lady Fothergill can't seem to get enough of it. She is a proud creature with an excessively sharp, barbed tongue. It would do her good to curb it a bit. Not that it matters, as she is about to unleash her weapon on the poor Viennese."

"What an apt description of Selena!" Not that Avery had ever seen her in the ballroom.

"And you remain at your brother's residence?" the lady enquired.

"Yes, but..." The door opened and a group of ladies entered, giggling, and chatting.

The lady released her hand. "I must return. I trust I shall see more of you in the future, Lady Avery." She nodded a friendly goodbye and left.

Avery returned to the ballroom elated. Whoever this beautiful, charming, and very talkative lady was, she was one of the few people in her life who'd truly seen her, if only for a moment. For the first time in her life, she'd made an acquaintance through her own efforts. Friends were few and far between in her life, so she cherished every friendly encounter.

"Oh, my goodness, there you are! I thought I'd lost you forever!" Belinda grabbed her arm. "I've been looking everywhere for you! Where have you been? Have you ever seen anything like this? Isn't this a terrible crush?" Her face was flushed, and she waved a peacock fan to cool herself.

"I was only in the lady's retirement room for a while."

"Next time I'll chain you to me so I don't lose you again!" Belinda scolded her.

"I'm quite ready to go home now," Avery told her.

"But the ball has only just begun, and you have not danced!"

"Yes, but with whom?"

"I thought I saw another acquaintance of ours earlier. Mr Theophil Carey."

"Never heard of him."

"He's your sister-in-law's uncle. Impossible to find anyone in this crowd, otherwise I would have introduced you, and I am sure he would have asked you to dance." Her eyes narrowed as she scanned the crowd.

Avery wondered if Belinda had made him up, or if she really did have a cousin called Theophil Carey. She examined the crowd, inadvertently looking for a lady with burgundy headwear and a huge feather, but it was impossible to identify anyone.

"Never mind, Belinda. I really have had enough. It is too hot here, there are too many people, and I feel one of my migraines coming on. Besides, I made a terrible cake out of myself earlier by stumbling into the dancers, and now I am no longer in the mood to dance."

Belinda fanned her with her fan. "This place is a bit over the top," she agreed. "A public ball like this is not the place to make your debut. You are right, enough for today. We shall withdraw and come up with another plan. The Season has only just begun! There will be so many other private balls, soirees, and routs to attend! You will see!"

Arm in arm, they left the ballroom, leaving Avery to wonder how on earth Belinda would acquire invitations to private balls when neither of them knew anyone of consequence.

Chapter Eight

"How was the ball, my lady?" Jerkins asked as he served breakfast the next morning.

Avery rubbed her forehead. She had a headache, even though she hadn't touched alcohol except for the tiny glass of cheap champagne she'd had at the ball yesterday. It must have been poor quality.

"Suffocating," she replied. "Overwhelming. Everything was too much. The room was too decorated, the champagne too cheap, the music too loud, the people too...high in the instep."

"That is regrettable. Although, it is said that public balls are apparently more relaxed than private ones." Jerkins seemed uncommonly talkative that morning.

"Indeed?" She couldn't imagine how starchy people could be at private balls if they were so insufferably arrogant at public ones. Except for her latest acquaintance, of course. She must be an exception.

"Have you ever been to a ball, Jerkins?"

"No, my lady."

"Not even at a simple assembly somewhere, I don't know, in the country?"

"No, my lady."

"That's a shame. Though I daresay you wouldn't like it, for it's a dreadful squeeze, and you can hardly turn without ramming someone with your elbow."

"It does sound unpleasant, my lady."

Avery played around with her fork. "Jerkins?"

"Yes, my lady?"

"I thought we agreed to leave out the my lady?"

"Did we, my lady?"

She thought about throwing her napkin at him, just to jostle him out of his placid demeanour. Instead, she crumpled it into a ball and sighed.

"The worst part is, I never even danced. Not one single dance." She stared bitterly at her plate of uneaten scrambled eggs. "What use is there of going to a ball and not being able to dance?"

"That's unfortunate indeed, my lady."

"I shall never go to another ball, Jerkins." She would cross that item off her list with finality. She would concentrate on other things on it, like going to Astley's Amphitheatre, or the theatre and opera house. Oh, and Vauxhall! And the menagerie of wild and wonderful animals in the Tower.

She would have to tell Cousin Belinda of her change of plans. Her mood improved considerably. Even if Cousin Belinda turned out to be an actress and a fraud, Avery was grateful to have a companion with whom to visit all these places. She'd grudgingly relented and agreed to have her move into the house, after Belinda had promised to respect her privacy and to be as unobtrusive a presence as possible.

"You will hardly notice I'm there," she'd promised.

"Where did you find Mrs Wimplethorpe, I wonder?" Avery looked at Jerkins from under her eyelashes.

"I did not find her, my lady. She learnt that you had stayed here after Lord Fothergill left and came to call, if I remember correctly."

"Yes. But who informed Mrs Wimplethorpe that I was here?"

"I really would not know, my lady." He was as straight-faced as ever, and the sunlight glinted off his glasses, so she could not make out the expression in his eyes. "But how fortunate that she is here. I believe some trunks of hers have already arrived. I shall have to see to her accommodation. She will arrive later in the evening."

Avery grumbled, "Very well, Jerkins. You may go."

He left, only to return shortly after. "This has just arrived, my lady." He handed her a silver platter with a letter on it.

She took the folded missive, wrinkling her forehead as she stared at the unfamiliar handwriting. Who could it be? Perhaps Great-Aunt Euphemia in Dorset, wondering why she hadn't arrived yet? Could she still write, being blind?

She knew her aunt was not living entirely alone, for she had a housemaid and a nurse taking care of her. Avery would have taken over the role of the nurse had she gone to Dorset. Until then, she knew her great-aunt was taken care of, and there was no immediate urgency for Avery to join her. However, she could not shake the pang of guilt that shot through her. She would have to write to her aunt sooner or later, explaining the situation.

But now, she had to deal with this particular correspondence.

Avery peered at the letter.

Save for the address, the sheet of paper was empty, but two little cards fell out.

Ladies' Voucher
Almack's
Deliver to
Lady Avery Heywood
Ticket for the balls
On the Wednesdays in November 1814.

IT WAS SEALED with a red dollop of wax and signed with an illegible scrawl in the bottom right-hand corner.

Avery's mouth fell open. Almack's? The most exclusive marriage mart in London? This had to be a joke.

"Jerkins," she handed him the voucher, "my eyes seem to be failing me. Perhaps it is time for me to get some spectacles, because I seem to imagine that this says 'Almack's'."

Jerkins took the card. "No need for spectacles just yet, my lady. It is indeed a genuine Almack's voucher."

"Good gracious!"

"Congratulations, my lady. This is the most coveted

item in the *ton*; everyone seeks a voucher, yet it is only given to a very select few."

Not even her brother and Selena had managed to acquire one. The patronesses presiding over who was granted a voucher were notoriously fastidious in their choices.

"But how? And why?"

"I believe another card fell out, my lady," Jerkins pointed out. "Perhaps it will provide more information."

He was right. On the tablecloth lay a small white calling card. In flourishing gold letters, it read,

Sarah Villiers, Countess of Jersey

Avery paled. "Jerkins. I feel ill." Her hand trembled as she handed him the card.

Both his eyebrows shot up. "Lady Jersey. One of the patronesses guarding the gates to the holy temple of Almack's." He turned the card over. "There's a short message on the back. Would you like me to read it to you?"

"Please." She wrung her hands.

"We expect to see you soon. Sally." Jerkins looked impressed. "The very first ball, and you are already on a first-name basis with one of the most powerful hostesses in the *ton*. You have received Lady Jersey's seal of approval. My heartiest congratulations, my lady! Your Season shall undoubtedly be a success."

"Lady Jersey!" Avery moaned.

Lady Jersey's reputation was legendary. She was admired, feared, adulated, and hated all at once. Fickle, beautiful, and immensely intelligent, she had the power to make or destroy a person's reputation in the beau monde. Nary a day passed without her appearing in the papers. An outraged husband once called out Lady Jersey's husband because she'd dared to refuse his wife a voucher. It was best not to cross Lady Jersey, or any of the other patronesses, for that matter, if one wanted to be admitted to the polite world.

Avery wished the freshly waxed parquet floor would open and swallow her whole. "The things I said to that woman! I called her a squirrel! After I told her she would look beautiful in a turnip sack!" She jumped up and down in agitation, wringing her hands.

"That is unfortunate." Jerkins's voice sounded oddly strangled.

"And then I tore off part of her dress!" Avery wailed. "I told her I didn't like it, and it must have cost half a fortune, and then I went and ruined it, in addition to her headwear, which now has a badly stitched ostrich feather on it that looks like a fox's tail."

Jerkins did not reply anything at all, but his face twitched.

"I suppose I must apologise to her, though in my defence, she seemed to be immensely pleased by my alterations to her dress. Do you think this is a summons to Almack's so she can humiliate me in front of her friends?" A small voice inside her said she had not seemed so spiteful, and that her behaviour had appeared sincere;

however, with Lady Jersey, one never knew. She had a reputation for being fickle.

Then something occurred to Avery. She sat down and took a deep breath. "'Anyhow, the point is moot. I cannot possibly go. I have no chaperone."

For Belinda would also need a voucher. It would be easier to propel the earth to spin the opposite way than to obtain an Almack's voucher for Belinda, who was, despite her claims to a connection to her family, a nobody.

"Besides, I would rather have all my teeth, toenails, and fingernails pulled than be a wallflower again and sit in the ignoble seats of shame watching everyone else dance. It is excessively humiliating and makes one feel that while one has been granted access to the holy temple of the *ton*, one is only allowed to watch from behind a glass wall, and not actually participate, because one lacks something." Avery brooded. "And one never entirely knows what that 'something' might be. It might be anything: the looks, the wrong age, the fashion. Maybe one is wearing the wrong-coloured gown. Maybe it's an unacceptable genealogy, or maybe it's something as simple as having sweaty feet and a pimple on your nose. In the end, it all comes down to someone like Lady Jersey, and whether she lifts or drops her thumb, Caligula-style, entirely on a whim, quite possibly depending on nothing more than what she has eaten for breakfast that may or may not have given her flatulence." She ended her monologue with a big sigh.

Jerkins uttered a strangled cough.

"In my case, she decided to lift the thumb because I happened to amuse her. I'm not sure it is worth entering the colosseum. As soon as she gets tired of me and realises I'm nothing but a tiresome old spinster, she'll drop her thumb, and I'll be thrown to the lions."

Jerkins, who had struggled to follow her rambling Roman analogy, drew his eyebrows together without losing his composure. "I beg your pardon, my lady. If I may be so bold as to interpret your words, you intend to decline Lady Jersey's invitation?"

"I know it's outrageous, but what else can I do?" Avery tugged at her earlobe, releasing her pearl earring. It had been a gift from her father. She held it between her fingers and stared at it. "Besides, if I go, I'll probably make a cake of myself again and fall into the orchestra and knock over a palm tree, or worse. Besides, I have nothing suitable to wear. And I refuse to go unless I have someone to dance with." She set her lips in a mulish line.

"But you can't possibly refuse this invitation. It would be unheard of. You must go." Jerkins was uncharacteristically insistent.

"Then why don't you go, if it means so much to you?" Avery replied petulantly. Then she stared at Jerkins, her eyes wide. "Oh, Jerkins! I've just had the most brilliant, fantastic idea! If you were to go to the ball and ask me to dance, then it would be different, wouldn't it? I would not be a wallflower; I would have someone to talk to other than Lady Jersey, who now frightens me to death, and it might turn out to be quite amusing after all. Except, of course, how would we go about getting you a voucher?"

Jerkins stared at her, appalled. "But I can't dance, my lady."

"You could learn."

He held up both hands to fend her off. "I'm afraid I must decline. Forgive me, but this is an outrageous idea."

"Yes, it is, isn't it? Shockingly outrageous. But wouldn't it be wonderful if it worked? It would solve all my problems! If you were to appear at every ball and rout and other event and ask me to dance and bring me drinks and be my escort, I am certain people would notice and then maybe, just maybe, other gentlemen would follow suit and ask me to dance as well. I promise you, I can dance very well indeed."

"I don't doubt that but apart from the voucher, the problem is that I'm pretending to be someone I'm not. It's not exactly moral, is it?"

"Piffle." Avery crossed her arms. "I have led a highly moral life, and look where it has got me. Besides, you hired an actress to play my cousin. I'm no fool, you know." She raised a finger to stop Jerkins as he parted his lips in protest. "Anyhow, it turned out to be a brilliant idea, and I rather like Mrs Wimplethorpe, even if she is an impostor. My point is, if Mrs Wimplethorpe can be my cousin, then you could be, I don't know." She snapped her fingers. "A cousin too, or better still, an uncle."

"Uncle?" Jerkins deigned to look offended. "Certainly not."

"Cousin, then."

Jerkins assessed her. "It's quite impossible, I'm afraid."

Avery sighed. "I know. I know. Let me indulge in a little fantasy for a moment."

"May I suggest that you inform Mrs Wimplethorpe of this matter and see if she has any suggestions? She may have some connections."

"I really don't think she knows anyone of any consequence, and I doubt very much that Belinda will be able to obtain an Almack's voucher herself." Avery thought. "Unless you know someone who can forge one?" Then she threw up her hands. "Forget I ever said that. You seem to have a corrupting influence on me, Jerkins."

"But if she could go, would you go?" he insisted.

Avery thought for a moment. "If she had a voucher too...I suppose I might. Just to see what it's like. But I'm not sure I would go without someone to dance with. Don't forget that chair of ignominy and shame."

Jerkins stood quietly by the window, a thoughtful frown on his face. "I can't make any promises, my lady," he finally said, so quietly that she thought she'd not heard correctly.

Avery jumped up with a squeak. "Does that mean you're going?"

"We shall have to see, my lady."

With a bow, he left.

Chapter Nine

"OF COURSE WE'RE GOING TO ALMACK'S!" BELINDA clapped her hands and jumped up and down, her bright copper curls bouncing. "Why haven't I thought of it myself? It's a wonderful idea."

They sat in the drawing room for tea, even though it was almost time for dinner, but Belinda had just risen from bed. True to her word, she'd been sleeping most of the day. Avery had to admit she looked fresh and pretty in her dark blue pelisse and matching bonnet.

"No, it's certainly not a wonderful idea, for how are we to get you in?" Avery began to regret the moment she had ever met Lady Jersey, who was solely to blame for this conundrum.

"But what could you possibly mean, Cousin? I have a voucher, so naturally I have purchased a subscription to this Season's balls." Belinda took a sip of her heavily sweetened tea.

Avery stared as Belinda set down her cup, picked up

a lemon tart and bit into it. Her tongue slipped over her pink lips to pick up the crumbs.

"You...have been given a voucher?"

"Of course I have."

"Of course you have," Avery echoed. "How silly of me to have assumed otherwise."

"Freddie—may his soul rest in peace—was a friend of Lady Emily Cowper's husband, the earl." Belinda finished her lemon tart and took another sip from her teacup. "Freddie and Peter have known each other since childhood, you see."

"I see," she said weakly. "Freddie is your husband, of course, and Peter is Lord Cowper, and Lady Emily Cowper is one of Almack's patronesses." It seemed she owed Belinda an apology for assuming she was an actress without connections.

"Indeed!" Belinda beamed at Avery. "The other patronesses are Ladies Castlereagh, Jersey, Sefton, the Princess Esterhazy, and Countess Lieven. You should have told me earlier that you had your sights on Almack's. I could have taken you as a guest. I am sure Emily would have approved, and she would have issued you a voucher at the snap of her fingers." She snapped her fingers to emphasise her point. "She is kindness in person, and not as sharp-tongued and arrogant as Lady Jersey or Princess Esterhazy."

"I did not find Lady Jersey arrogant or sharp-tongued at all. But she certainly liked to talk."

"That she does! Did you know that her nickname is 'Silence'?"

Avery smiled involuntarily. "That is apt."

"But it is excellent that Lady Jersey has issued you a voucher. You must have impressed her in some manner."

Avery pulled a face. "I must have, indeed."

Belinda leaned forward as if confiding a secret. "Though you must be warned: Almack's is a dreadfully dull affair. The refreshments are inedible, and the drinks are, to put it mildly, abysmal. They serve no alcohol at all, therefore many young gentlemen are reluctant to attend, and must be forced to by their mothers. Almack's is the central marriage mart, so the prime aim is to find a suitable partner to marry. As a result, there is something about the atmosphere that seems perpetually forced and tense. If you ask me, people are just trying too hard to tie the knot. I daresay we would be better off entertaining ourselves at a masquerade in the Argyle Rooms. But now that you have made Lady Jersey's acquaintance and she has approved of you, we shall of course go to Almack's, for after all, it is the place to be, and we shall do our best to have a jolly good time there. But first we must see to the matter of your wardrobe." She gave Avery an appraising look.

Avery sighed. "That's another matter. I can't wear any more of my sister-in-law's clothes; they're hopelessly out of date."

"Don't worry, I know just where to go. Madame Minion. She will make you the most beautiful dresses in the latest fashion. Let us go immediately." Belinda wiped the crumbs off her lap and stood.

Avery raised both hands. "I'm sorry to dampen your enthusiasm, Cousin, but my pockets aren't plump enough to afford a fashionable dressmaker." It was well known that many a lady had emptied her coffers down to the last penny just to have a gown made according to the latest crack.

"Say no more, I understand perfectly, Cousin. Since my Freddie passed away—may his soul rest in peace—and left my own coffers far from lined, I have had to resort to certain means and measures to help me maintain my own wardrobe. A lady simply needs certain items to survive in this world. And a decent dress is one of them. We shall venture forth immediately. But be warned, we may have to pass through some unsavoury parts of the city to reach the shop I have in mind."

To CALL THE ROOKERY 'UNSAVOURY' was an understatement if ever there was one. It was a district of London where even Bow Street runners hesitated to venture. St Giles consisted of a maze of squalid, dirty, and dangerous streets inhabited by the impoverished, prostitutes, bands of thieves, highwaymen, and other criminals.

"I do not know whether it's a good idea to drive through this area," Avery told Belinda with a nervous tremor. "They might hold up the carriage and attempt to rob us."

"Never fear. We will not be going through, just passing by. There is a warehouse on Giles High Street, and they are expecting us. My footman will accompany us into the house, and he has a pistol. Nothing will happen, you will see."

A warehouse in St Giles. Avery wrinkled her nose.

This could not be a normal warehouse, but most likely a place where illegal goods were sold. Probably smuggled goods.

Avery gave her an alarmed look. "You're not suggesting anything unlawful, are you?"

Belinda laughed. "Oh no, far from it! But come with me and I will show you."

She leaned back and watched Belinda thoughtfully. At first, Avery had been so convinced she was an actress hired by Jerkins that it hadn't occurred to her that she might indeed be Mrs Wimplethorpe, with some tenuous relationship to her. If Belinda's husband had indeed been friends with Lord Cowper, then she'd misjudged her, and she must be who she said she was after all. But now Belinda was taking her into one of the most dangerous areas of London, with a cheerful expression on her face, as if this was something she did every day.

Doubt nagged at the back of Avery's mind again. What if she was a hired actress after all, rubbing shoulders with smugglers of illegal goods? What proper lady would ever venture into St Giles to buy fabric?

The coach stopped. Just as Belinda had said, the footman opened the door, a pistol in his hand. He led them into a dilapidated warehouse with only the name Smith's on the front. A seedy-looking man greeted them inside and led them through a maze of corridors to a room with darkened windows. The armed footman followed close behind.

Avery gripped Belinda's arm. Belinda patted her hand reassuringly. "Here we are. Good afternoon, Mr Smith. We have come to inspect the latest silks."

They had arrived in a large room with open crates and tables on which were mountains of bolts of fabric in every conceivable colour and texture. Several men were opening boxes at one end of the room and heaving the bolts onto the tables, and a woman was sorting them by colour. None of them stopped working when they entered, except for a thin man in a brown coat who was bending over a crate. He straightened up to greet them. "Mrs Wimplethorpe. Welcome! And I see you have brought a new customer."

"We're looking for the finest, latest sarsenet, preferably embroidered. What do you have to offer?"

Mr Smith swept his eyes over the tables. "We have, newly arrived from India, this brown silk embroidered with green leaves." He unrolled a bolt and let the brown fabric glide across the table. "I have just learned that the Duchess of Meringbroke purchased this very fabric. Note that this is exactly the same silk, except the leaves are facing the wrong way."

"In what way is it wrong?" Avery stared at a row of beautifully embroidered green leaves facing each other.

The man pointed to the top of one leaf. "This one should be facing the other way. It is a tiny manufacturing error that no one will ever notice. Nevertheless, this bolt has been discarded because it cannot be sold in the fashionable warehouses."

"They are left for people like us to buy at a quarter of the original price, and no one will ever notice the difference." Belinda beamed at him. "What would I do without you, Mr Smith?"

He bowed. "Always at your service, madam."

Avery sighed with relief. Not smuggled goods after all, but bolts of cloth sold cheaply because of minor flaws.

Belinda fingered the fabric. "Lovely. But the colour is too dark for you." She held the fabric in Avery's face. "Makes you look very pale. Methinks we need something lighter for my cousin."

"Yes, not brown." Avery remembered Lady Jersey's comments. "A strong cobalt blue or emerald green. But what I would like most is red."

"Red. Very well, madam. What shade shall it be? I have hibiscus, maroon, and Persian red on offer today," Mr Smith said.

"Show us all three," Belinda demanded.

Mr Smith hoisted the bolts onto the table for them to inspect.

In the end they bought enough fabric for three new ball gowns each. Avery chose the Persian red with a sapphire blue and emerald-green silk satin, while Belinda chose the brown with green embroidered leaves with a heavier mauve velvet.

"This will look fantastic with a purple turban," she explained. Avery could just imagine her in it.

Satisfied with her purchases, Avery stepped back into the carriage.

"I always buy my fabric there," Belinda said as the carriage set off. "Then it is easier to afford the dressmaker. But knowing Madame Minion, she will give us a good price, especially if I bring her a new customer."

Belinda chatted on, but Avery no longer heard what she said. She stared out of the carriage window as it clattered along the High Street, passing St Giles Rookery on the left. As the coach stopped to let a costermonger pass, Avery caught a glimpse of a narrow, crammed side street, squalid beyond words. People lay begging in the gutter, drunk or dead. The foul stench in the air was appalling. But what caught Avery's attention was a group of sloppily dressed men emerging from a gin shop. They looked as if they belonged to a criminal gang. One of them, a short, bulky fellow with a battered hat, was slapping the shoulders of a taller man in a shabby black coat and handing something to one of the other men. His hat was pulled low over his forehead and his shoulders were pulled up and slightly stooped. As he turned sideways, Avery caught sight of his profile.

That eagle-like nose.

That chin!

She gasped.

Then the carriage began to move. Avery pressed her face against the window, but she lost sight of the men.

She fell back into her seat, her head spinning.

Belinda, who was still talking about the silks, interrupted herself to ask, "Is anything the matter?"

She shook her head. "It's the strangest thing. I thought I saw someone I knew."

"Here? I'd say that's highly unlikely." Belinda's eyes shifted away. "You must be mistaken."

"Precisely what I am thinking," Avery replied. "Tell me, what sort of person would visit a squalid gin shop in the rookery in the middle of the day with a group of seedy-looking individuals? And for what purpose?"

"Someone up to no good," Belinda replied promptly. "The gin shop on the corner is known to be a hotbed of criminal activity. It's the haunt of brigands and outlaws. No decent person would set foot in there. And do you see that inn over there?" She pointed to a public house across the street. "That's the Angel Inn. It's where the condemned can have their last bowl of ale on their way to the gallows. At least they used to, back when they were hanged at Tyburn. Now they all swing outside Newgate without the parade through the city."

The coachman had told her the same the other day. Avery swallowed. "You seem to know an awful lot about this area," she said casually.

Belinda's eyes shifted again. "I only visit the warehouse, and one can't help but hear all sorts of gossip," she murmured. "But tell me, who did you see?"

Avery waved her away. "I must have imagined it. It was just a trick of the eye, I am sure."

Yet she could have sworn on the wig of their mad king that that man she had seen had been no one else but Jerkins.

Chapter Ten

"WHERE'S JERKINS?" AVERY ASKED THE NEW housemaid, who opened the door.

"He has left to run some errands, my lady." The new girl took her pelisse, bonnet, and gloves.

"Please excuse me. I'll retire for a nap," Belinda yawned and made her way up the staircase.

Avery went to the study and sat down at her brother's desk, her brows knitted together in a deep frown.

Since when did butlers run errands?

That was the role of footmen.

Butlers were the head of the male staff, ruling almost like kings over the servants beneath them. Their roles were strictly defined, and as far as she knew, butlers never cooked, cleaned, or ran errands. Their job was to intimidate guests, count bottles of wine in the cellar, count more silverware and china, in addition to merging into the wallpaper and just...hovering there. Must be a dreadfully humdrum life, she concluded. Therefore, if one had a dull occupation like that, it was entirely reasonable to assume one might be overcome by an overwhelming craving to break out of one's role and make excursions...into the rookery.

Avery pinched her lower lip between two fingers.

Yet Jerkins wasn't an ordinary kind of butler. She'd caught him breaking out of his role several times within the first week of her stay alone in Wimpole Street. He'd already cooked for her on the first day, and he hadn't been above himself to tidy up the study. Then the other day, she'd caught him dusting the Chinese vase in the drawing room. He had been wearing an apron, and he had a napkin tied around his head that made him look like a milkmaid. Avery, who'd walked past the drawing room, had paused, blinked, and retraced her steps.

"What on earth are you wearing on your head, Jerkins?"

"A protection against dust, my lady."

"I see." She'd stared. "Pray, carry on."

"Yes, my lady."

So, it should come as no surprise to her that he was running errands as well.

In a gin shop in one of the most squalid areas of London, where criminals and misfits dwelled.

She really ought not to harp on it too much. Yet the people he associated with had certainly not inspired any kind of trust.

Avery plucked at the feathers of her quill. Rather disquieting how he'd appeared to be one of them.

A feeling of unease took hold of her.

What did she really know about Jerkins? Where did he come from, and what had he done before he'd become a butler? He'd never worked at Penmaron Hall but had been hired when her brother Tom and his family had rented the townhouse in London. He'd come with the house. Stevens, the butler at Penmaron Hall, had grown old and retired at around the same time, so it had been convenient that Jerkins had been so readily available. She'd never seen his references. What did she know about what he did all day? Why had he decided to stay alone in the townhouse instead of joining the other servants after Tom and his family had left? And ultimately, did any of this really matter?

She shrugged. Maybe she ought to mind her own business. So far, she'd had no reason to complain as he performed his duties conscientiously and punctiliously.

In any case, she had more important things to do than wonder about what her butler did in his free time. She pulled out a piece of paper and wrote:

The Story of the Debonair Highwayman.

She stared at the words, then crossed them out with firm strokes. Dashing? Venturesome? Audacious? Tenacious? Bold?

Somehow none of these words fit.

After a moment she wrote:

The Story of the Dashing Highwayman.

THAT WAS SLIGHTLY BETTER, but still not right. She crossed it out again.

The Story of the Intrepid Highwayman.

Better.

A dashing highwayman rode down the moonlit road. The moon shone in the black night sky, for there were no stars.

Bah! What drivel was this? She'd mentioned the moon in the first sentence, no need to repeat it in the second. Besides, if there was a moon bright enough to illuminate the road, the night couldn't have been that black.

She crumpled the paper into a small ball and threw it on the floor and started anew.

After two hours, she looked up with a frustrated sigh.

Writing was difficult! Why was telling stories to the boys easier and more enjoyable than writing them down?

After another half-hour of wrestling with her writing, a growing mountain of little balls on the floor next to her, Avery leaned back in the chair with a groan.

"No, no, no. This is terrible. I don't know what Jerkins was thinking, suggesting I could ever put one of my stories down on paper." It was like pulling teeth. She reread what she'd written, shook her head, crumpled the paper, and threw it across the room into the fireplace.

Instead of landing in the grate, it hit one of Tom's precious Ming vases on the mantelpiece, which began to topple dangerously.

"Oh no!" Avery shot out of the chair and caught the vase just in time. "That was close." She set the vase back, then bent down to pick up the paper ball.

Her gaze fell into the unlit grate, travelled up—and stopped.

In the side wall of the fireplace, almost in the chimney, a strange brick stood out. It wasn't sooty like the rest of the bricks around it, but red. Almost as if someone had dusted it.

Without much ado, Avery reached in, grabbed it, and pulled it out with ease.

Her heart pounded. There was an opening behind it! She reached in and pulled out a small package.

It was a small leather notebook wrapped in an oilcloth. Avery turned it in her hands and opened the leather straps tied around it. The book was filled with neat handwriting. A list of some sort, with dates.

May 2, 1790
A purse of coins, a necklace of pearls.
May 25
A sovereign, two leather gloves, a pair of emerald earrings.
June 3
25 gold coins.
June 7
A pocket watch, two gold cufflinks.
June 14
Two kisses.

Two kisses? How excessively odd and out of place. Avery turned the pages in confusion. The entire notebook was filled with dates and random items. What did it mean? Was this Tom's? Why would he hide it in the fireplace?

No, it couldn't be Tom's. The dates inside were from long before they'd even moved into the townhouse. 1790.

She opened it to the beginning and stared at the initials on the first page.

JT.

Her stomach flipped. She'd seen those initials before, on the pistol she'd handled yesterday.

Avery sat down heavily in the chair.

This was a notebook belonging to Jax Tyrrell.

What on earth was it doing in this house? Who had hidden it there?

As she stared at the endless list of items recorded, it dawned on her that she was staring at Jax Tyrrell's list of spoils.

This was too strange. It was one thing for Tom to have Jax Tyrrell's pistol in his collection. It was quite another for him to have the highwayman's notebook in which he'd recorded his loot.

But why would Tom hide it? The man was long dead.

Unless, of course, Tom had nothing to do with this notebook.

She leafed through it again, noting the pretty, almost feminine handwriting. The I's were dotted, and the Y's had lovely curlicues.

No, Tom must have known. He must have obtained the notebook together with the pistol and hidden it in his chimney.

For whatever reason.

Avery's imagination ran wild.

What sort of man had Jax Tyrrell been? Was he as wild and romantic as the legends claimed? They said he'd been a gentleman highwayman who'd never shed any blood. He'd been gallant to the ladies, stealing kisses from them while he robbed their husbands.

Was that the meaning of "two kisses"?

What a mystery that man was.

She stared at the few meagre sentences she'd written about the Intrepid Highwayman. If she could only find out more about a real highwayman, like Jax Tyrrell, maybe that would help her write the story.

She was already in possession of his pistol, and now his list of booty. Belinda had mentioned an Inn in St Giles that had been the haunt of highwaymen...something with an Angel. It was a shame she was still sleeping.

An idea formed in her mind.

She jumped up, rang the bell, and ordered her abigail, Emma, to call for a hackney.

"Oh, and Emma, I need a plain, dark cloak, and get one for yourself too. You are to accompany me."

Emma threw her a quick look of surprise. "Yes, my lady."

Avery rubbed her hands gleefully. She had some investigating to do.

Chapter Eleven

AVERY HAD NEVER SET FOOT IN A PUBLIC HOUSE before.

Another thing to cross off her list!

Yet it was with some trepidation that she lifted her skirt and crossed the threshold of the Angel Inn in St Giles.

Emma grabbed her sleeve. "Forgive me, my lady, but I'm not sure this is a good idea. This is a bad place." She glanced around the dark and smoky room. "This is the haunt of thieves and cadgers. Nothing good will come of it."

"Nonsense, Emma. Nothing will happen if we stay together. I just need to ask the innkeeper a few questions, that's all. We'll be in and out in no time."

The walls of the pub were all black, some from soot and some from dark wood panelling. A fire blazed in the hearth, and though it was midday, the place was full of shabby-looking characters sitting at tables and drinking.

The smell of sour ale, boiled cabbage, and sweat assaulted her.

Avery marched to the bar, where a short, bald man in a dirty apron was polishing glasses with a dirty rag tied around his pot belly. Emma followed, clinging to her.

"Are you the landlord?" Avery demanded.

"Aye. How can I be of service to two lovely ladies?" The landlord looked her over with his small, dark, beady eyes. No doubt he could tell at a glance that she was Quality, but he remained unimpressed.

"I just need some information, if you please." Avery pulled out a pen and notebook.

"In'fo'mah-tion." The man mimicked her pronunciation, crossed his arms over his broad chest and grinned, revealing a set of blackened teeth. "Ma'am wants in'fo'mah-tion."

"Aye." Emma pushed herself in front of Avery. "That's after you've served us a pint, for each of us."

Emma's voice had changed completely, and she spoke in the same broad accent as the innkeeper. Avery gave her a surprised look.

Emma pushed several coins across the counter, then started to stack another pile of coins. "Well?"

"Well, lass," the innkeeper grinned, "in that case, you'll find me a veritable fountain of in'fo'ma-tion." He pushed two black mugs of ale towards them.

Emma nodded at Avery to take one. She nipped at the brew and pulled a face. The brew was hideous.

"Well? I'm waiting." The innkeeper crossed his arms. "Ask away."

Avery set down her mug. "This is such a famous inn, I hear. So, err, distinguished and respectable."

The man grinned. "That she is, me angel." He rubbed his hand over the counter as if caressing it. "A coaching inn like no other." His little finger was a mere stub.

Avery stared at it, fascinated, then looked away. "And so conveniently situated halfway between Newgate and Tyburn."

"Aye. We're a conveniently situated inn."

"So, you must have seen many famous scoundrels pass by here on their way to the gallows."

"Aye, I have. The poor devils tend to stop here for their last bowl before they swing."

"I'm just curious, Mr..."

"Purkiss."

"Mr Purkiss. How many famous highwaymen have passed through here?"

Purkiss raised an eyebrow at Emma, who was putting another coin on top of the stack.

He shrugged. "All of em, I say. Jack Sheppard, Tom Cox, John Nevison. This house has seen 'em all."

"Yes, but they all lived and died in the last century. What about more recently? What about Jax Tyrrell?"

Was she imagining it or did a hush fall over the taproom?

A lurking glance flitted over his face. "Now that's a name one better not utter out loud."

"But he's dead."

"Aye, and he'd better be."

"Can't you tell me anything about him?" Avery pressed, pencil ready.

"There's nothing to say. He was a highwayman, he was caught, kicked the bucket, end of story."

"Yes, but he must have stopped here for his last draught. Did you see him? What did he look like? What did he say?"

He shrugged.

"Do you think he kept track of all the items he robbed?" Avery carried the little notebook in her reticule, so maybe it was a redundant question. But she wanted to see how the innkeeper reacted.

He narrowed his beady eyes at her so they seemed almost closed. "Maybe he did, maybe he did not. What's it to you? And why would a lady want to know about Jax Tyrrell, after all this time?"

"I'm just interested, that's all."

He continued to stare at her, deadpan, and no matter the amount of coins Emma piled on, he would not open his mouth.

Avery sighed. "The truth is, I'm writing a story, and I need to do some research. It would be more realistic if I could penetrate the legend and learn more about the actual man behind it."

The man's face closed as if someone had slammed the wooden shutters on the shop windows. "You're a bleedin' journalist writing for the papers?"

"Well, not exactly—"

"Out! I'm not talking to nobody writing for the papers. This is an honourable inn, and I don't want no attention brought to this here house." His voice had grown to a roar.

"But—"

"No one will write about this inn," Emma said hastily, taking Avery's arm. "We'd better go." She pulled her towards the door.

A shadowy figure sucking on a pipe emerged from the shadows of a corner and grabbed Emma's arm. "Weel, weel, weel, if this ain't pretty little Hetty Wiles as I live and die. Thought me eyes are playin' me tricks but here ye are, wily little thing that ye are. Haven't seen ye hereabouts in a while. Always been handy with a knife, I remember, that's why they call ye 'Stabbing Hetty'," he chuckled loudly. "Escaped from gaol after stabbing the warden?" He flashed a mouth of revolting black teeth at her.

Emma recoiled. "You mistake me for someone else."

"Risen above yer station, have ye? Rubbing shoulders with the nobs." He shot Avery a malevolent glare. She shrank back. "Too good to talk to old Mac now. But always remember," he raised a grimy finger in the air, "once born in the rookery, always the rookery. Ye can't never escape it."

His cackle of laughter followed them long after they'd scrambled into the coach and left.

"Who on earth was that?" Avery gasped.

"I don't know, my lady. Dreadful old man. He mistook me for someone else." Emma's face was ashen.

"Well, you spoke their language quite well..." Avery's voice trailed off. "Were you brought up in the rookery, Emma?"

"No, my lady. I swear it." Her eyes shifted away from hers, and Avery had the nagging feeling that she was lying.

"Well." She frowned down at her notebook, which was woefully empty. "That wasn't very productive, was it? I thought the innkeeper might have wanted to brag a bit more about his encounter with the legendary highwayman before he was hanged. But he was strangely tight-lipped about it."

"My lady, Purkiss never met Jax Tyrrell because he never stopped at the Angel Inn on his way to Tyburn. I could have told you that myself."

"But why not? Purkiss himself said that every criminal stopped there for his last drink, and he was very proud of it."

"Yes, but not Jax Tyrrell. He never did."

"But he was brought in from Newgate, wasn't he?" Avery pressed.

"Yes, and a crowd as big as ever followed his coach."

"But he never stopped at the Angel?" Avery shook her head. "Why? Don't you find it strange that he didn't want to talk about Jax Tyrrell at all? He was the most famous of all highway robbers."

"Does it matter, my lady?"

"I just find it odd, that's all."

Neither of them had noticed another shadowy figure in another corner who'd been eagerly following their conversation in the tavern. He crept out of the shadows, emptied his pipe against the wall, and spat on the floor as he watched the coach round the bend and disappear from sight.

Chapter Twelve

"WHERE DID YOU SAY YOU WERE, MY LADY?"

Jerkins's voice lashed through the silence like steel. Emma had thrown him a frightened look and stolen away, mumbling she had things to do, leaving Avery standing in the foyer, facing Jerkins on her own. He was clearly unamused.

She tugged on the strings of her bonnet and immediately regretted she'd told him about this morning's excursion. She'd never suspected that the imperturbable, gentle-mannered Jerkins could get so formidable.

She raised her chin defiantly. "To St Giles." She took off the bonnet and handed it to him. "It was nothing. Just a quick trip to an inn. The new girl Emma was with me, of course." Then she focused on removing her gloves with concentration, so she did not have to meet his ice-cold gaze.

"Are you aware that St Giles is the most dangerous district of London? That it is a hotbed of crime? And that one does not simply stroll around for a visit?" He spoke so quietly and softly that it was fairly terrifying. He was her butler, dash it, and had no business reprimanding her as if she were a stammering schoolgirl caught stealing a jar of sugar plums from the pantry.

"Well, to be precise, we weren't exactly strolling about in the little streets of the rookery, just on St Giles High Street. We were visiting a public house. The Angel Inn, to be exact. For research. Not that that's any of your business, Jerkins," she added for good measure. She would not tell him this was her second visit to that disreputable area and that she'd imagined seeing him there, too. It lay on her lips to ask whether it had indeed been him, but something told her this was not a good moment to mention it.

Jerkins closed his eyes for an infinitesimal second, as if struggling for composure. Or patience. Or both.

"The Angel Inn is a notorious haunt for burglars, thieves, and criminals of all kinds," he snapped. "Are you aware you have placed yourself in great danger and that you could have been robbed, kidnapped, or worse? Are you aware that someone may have followed you home and now knows where you live?"

The thought rattled her. "Nonsense, Jerkins. Whyever would they do that? As you can see, I am here, perfectly well, and not a hair on my head has been harmed. Besides, it really is beyond the pale that you're telling me what I can and cannot do." She raised her chin belligerently.

"In the absence of your brother or any other male relative to care for you, the responsibility for your safety and well-being has fallen on my shoulders. And I tend to guard that responsibility well."

For a moment, Avery groped for words. "You absolutely do not have that responsibility!" she replied after she'd found her tongue. "We are not related, and I am not a child to be guarded." She felt like stomping on the ground to prove her point, only to realise she would only achieve the opposite.

Something flared in his eyes. "Let us be clear on one thing, my lady. As long as you live here, you are under my care and protection. That is not up for debate."

Avery threw up her hands. "Oh, look at us quarrelling. But really, you are taking this far too seriously and worrying too much. Nothing will happen to me."

"No. I'll make sure of that." His eyes flicked over her.

Her heart made a funny lurch. She swallowed and looked away. There was no point in arguing with Jerkins. He was as inflexible as an iron bar.

"Do you require my service in another matter, my lady?" he enquired with awful civility.

"No, thank you. I do not wish to be disturbed for the next few hours." She dismissed him with hauteur. "That includes Mrs Wimplethorpe."

"Mrs Wimplethorpe is out on a visit," he informed her.

True to her promise, she barely saw Belinda, even though they were now residing within the same house.

Avery was cross with Jerkins the entire afternoon and locked herself into the study to work on her story. But it would not come. She could not get Jerkins out of her

mind; how he'd looked at her with that look of exasperation, ire, and a hint of—possessiveness?

She dropped the quill and it made splotches on the
paper.

Surely, she'd been imagining things. But interesting
how her pulse increased at the mere thought of him.

She shook those thoughts away and focused on her
writing.

After several hours, she ran out of paper and ink.

When she pulled the bell, she braced herself for
another encounter with Jerkins.

But no one came.

It was a novelty for Avery, pulling a bell and no one
coming. Then she recalled Jerkins telling her earlier that
the bellpull in the study was broken and that it would be
fixed anon, except she hadn't paid attention because her
mind had still been in St Giles. She would have to go to
another room and pull the bell there. She stepped out
into the hallway and listened. Save for the clock ticking,
the house was oddly silent. Belinda was sleeping. And
the servants? Where was Emma? Or should she call her
'Stabbing Hetty'? What about the new housemaid? Did
she have a similar nickname?

Where was Jerkins when one needed him? Had he
slipped off to St Giles again? She was certain she'd not
made a mistake when she thought she saw him there.

Where on earth was the man?

No matter. She had no appetite for another meeting
with him. She would simply have to find paper and ink
on her own.

It couldn't be that difficult.

Where would it be stored?

Avery decided that below stairs was the place she was most likely to find it.

She waited a moment, then stepped up to the door leading down to the servants' quarters in the basement.

Once in the basement, the still room was to her left and the wine cellar to the right. The kitchen, scullery, and servants' hall were down the corridor to the left. Down the corridor to the right was the butler's pantry, the housekeeper's room, and at the end, the butler's room.

Everything was strangely quiet.

Avery stood at the closed door and knocked.

No one answered.

She opened the door.

I am not really trespassing, Avery told herself as she entered, for as the lady of the house she had every right to be here.

The room was disappointingly plain.

There was a narrow iron bed against the wall, a walnut chest of drawers with a jug and a pitcher on top, and a simple wardrobe.

His livery hung on the half-open wardrobe door.

Avery peered in and saw a brown coat hanging. She would not stoop so low as to go through his socks and shirts; that was uncalled for, indeed.

She picked up the bottle of cologne next to the pitcher. She opened it and smelled—bergamot, musk, and citron. Masculine and tangy, undoubtedly Jerkins's signature scent.

Avery smiled and returned it.

There was really nothing else in the room.

It was bare, undecorated, and there wasn't anything in particular to see.

Beside the bed stood a small nightstand. The first drawer was half open. She pulled it open and peered inside.

Her head spinning, she pulled it out further and stared.

There lay a flintlock pistol.

The rascal! Pretending he didn't even know how to hold a gun, and then he had one lying just like it next to his bed.

It was the twin of the other flintlock she'd used on the poor cherry tree several days ago.

Perhaps that was not surprising: duelling pistols came in pairs, and Jerkins had the key to the gun cabinet, so he'd taken the second one.

She pushed the drawer shut.

In the bottom drawer was a well-thumbed book of verse, which Avery took out curiously.

Poems by Byron.

Who could have known? Jerkins was a romantic.

She turned the pages, and a lock of hair fell out. White blonde, tied with a red bow.

Avery picked it up. It lay softly in the palm of her hand.

An old love of his? It had never occurred to her that he could have feelings for a woman. Did he have a sweetheart? Was it an old love he pined for? How odd—the woman's hair must be quite similar to her own.

Avery put it back and proceeded to leaf through the pages of the book.

He'd underlined some verses and added comments in the margins. How sweet.

A heart whose love is innocent, Byron had written.

Not only that, but pure, divine, he'd scribbled in beautiful cursive next to it.

She gasped.

Impossible! It was the same handwriting as in the notebook.

Avery pulled it out of her bag.

There was no doubt.

Both were in the penmanship of the same writer. The same curlicues, the same flourishes.

But how? And why?

Avery turned back to the title page. Her stomach plunged into the netherworld.

There it was—the same initials: JT.

Chapter Thirteen

"WHERE HAVE YOU BEEN, JERKINS? I MISSED YOU."
Avery marvelled that she was able to spoon her pea soup
with steady hands. She was having supper on her own,
since Belinda had said she had to visit a relative and
would return late.

Jerkins served the meal with his usual placid
demeanour and gave no indication at all he was a former
legendary highwayman returned from the dead.

She was burning to ask how he'd managed to do it,
given that half of London had seen him hanged, and his
body ought to be fodder for the worms six feet beneath
Hounslow Heath.

Avery grimaced. Not exactly an appetising thought
when one was having supper.

"I've been running errands, my lady."

That's right. It all came together. He'd been meeting
his fellow criminals in St Giles.

Avery dropped the spoon and speckled the white
damask tablecloth with green flecks of pea soup.

She took a deep breath and turned to him with a bright smile. "Indeed? What kind of errands?"

Selling Tom's silverware, in all likelihood. Irksome that only Jerkins knew how many spoons and knives there were in the household. She would have to make it a point of interest to count the silver and china herself from now on.

"I have had some trouble finding a suitable footman through our usual agency, given the general shortage of servants on the market, so I have had to take more unorthodox measures to find one."

"What unorthodox measures do you mean? Did you have to kidnap someone or force them at g-gunpoint? But then I forgot. You don't like guns, do you?"

Jerkins smiled. "I certainly do not, my lady. Domestics are very difficult to find these days. I would rather not expound upon the peculiars, but suffice it to say I was successful, and we shall have a footman starting tomorrow morning. He may not have any references, but I have it on good authority that he is a reliable, honest, hard-working person."

Sweet heavens. He'd hired another criminal!

Avery swallowed.

In addition to a charlatan companion and a high-wayman butler, she would now have a scallywag for a footman. Not to mention 'Stabbing Hetty.' Who knows? Maybe she really was a murderess. It was clear that Jerkins—she simply could not call him Jax, not even in her head—was planning to turn her brother's townhouse into a den of thieves. Avery made a mental note to move the commode in front of her door before she went to bed.

For good measure, she would smuggle one of the flint-locks out of Tom's cabinet and place it under her pillow.

As she took a sip from her wine glass, her hand finally shook. She set the glass down and wiped her perspiring fingers on her napkin.

"I have wondered, Jerkins, since we are talking about hiring domestic servants. From what agency did you say my brother hired you?" She grabbed the knife and made a show of sawing her slab of meat on the plate, peering at him from under her lashes. If attacked, she'd have to hurl the knife for lack of a better weapon.

He neither flinched nor made any other suspicious movement that gave away who he really was.

He raised an eyebrow. "Lord Fothergill never had to go to an agency to hire me."

Avery almost choked on her beefsteak. "He didn't?"

"No. I was Lord Blackshurst's man before I entered Lord Fothergill's service."

"Lord Blackshurst! Who is he?" The name was vaguely familiar, but she could not put a face to it.

"Lord Blackshurst is the current owner of this house, my lady. He is abroad at present, which was why he allowed Lord Fothergill to rent his residence."

"In other words, you were here before we came." She pointed her knife at him.

"Indeed, my lady. I have been in Lord Blackshurst's service for nearly eleven years."

"And how long have you been with us?"

"Nigh on three years, my lady."

"Three years." She drew an absent-minded pattern on the tablecloth with the blunt tip of her knife. This meant that he'd been hiding in the butler's guise, first with Lord Blackshurst, then in her brother's household, for nearly fourteen years. When was Jax Tyrrell hanged? She would have to work out if that added up. If it did, it was a clever trick indeed. A highwayman disguised as a butler.

What a story that would make!

Jerkins picked up her half-empty plate and said, "For pudding, we have a choice of vanilla custard with blackberries or your favourite, lemon tart. I presume it is to be the latter?"

Lemon tart was indeed her favourite. She could have lemon tart for breakfast, luncheon, tea, and supper. But Avery had lost all her appetite.

"Thank you, but no pudding for me tonight. I will retire early today, as tomorrow is Wednesday." Tomorrow would bring a whole new set of problems.

Jerkins nodded in understanding. "Almack's."

Her stomach churned at the thought. Her dress was ready, and unless Emma murdered her in her sleep, she would dress her hair tomorrow, and Belinda the beautiful charlatan would accompany her to the ball, while Jerkins and the new footman cheerfully plundered the house.

"Thank you, Jerkins." Avery nodded dismissively and turned to return to the study for another round of writing.

"Your ladyship." Jerkins's voice sounded unexpectedly commanding.

"Yes?"

"If I may be so bold as to request that you inform me directly whenever you are in need of something. It shall,

of course be provided, without you having to go extra
lengths to search for it."

She blinked at him. "I don't understand. Of course, I'll
ask—oh!"

"The area below the stairs is not at all appropriate for
a lady," he added gently.

A hot wave of embarrassment crept up her neck.

"I was just, er, looking for, for—paper! Yes, paper. You
know, to write on. I've used up every scrap there is in the
study, and I was desperate to find some more."

That wasn't even a lie. She'd buried the Persian rug
under a layer of paper balls.

"And ink!" she blurted out. "I need ink too. You
wouldn't happen to have any ink down there, would you?
All I found was turpentine and boot-black, and I can
hardly write with either, can I?"

Blimey, she was babbling nonsense.

Jerkins smiled benignly. "We'll see that you get all the
paper and ink you need, my lady."

"Yes, because this is turning out to be quite an
exciting story. The boys would have loved it. It is about a
swashbuckling highwayman who is about to rob a coach."
Her eyes widened as they fell on Jerkins, imagining him
in a mask on a horse.

"I'm sure it will be another one of your brilliant
stories."

"Most certainly. Would you like to read it?" Good
heavens, where did that come from? She hadn't meant to
blurt that out.

Jerkins looked pleased. "Indeed, I would, my lady. I've
always enjoyed your stories."

Perhaps it wasn't the worst idea. Maybe he could give her some input that would help her make her stories more realistic. After all, he was the one who'd actually experienced it. Besides, if she kept him busy like this, he could not come up with other ideas, like looting the house.

Excitement rushed through her.

She went to the study to collect her manuscript and handed it to Jerkins.

"This is precious to me, so take good care of it," she warned him.

He put his hand to his heart. "I will. It's an honour, my lady."

That night, as Avery lay in her bed with the washstand in front of her door (the chest of drawers had proved impossible to move) and a pistol under her pillow, she decided that perhaps it was not so bad that Jerkins was a former highwayman, for she could make use of his criminal knowledge.

Provided she did not find herself murdered in her own bed first.

Chapter Fourteen

THE NEXT MORNING, AVERY REALISED WITH SOME relief that she had not been murdered in her sleep when she woke up to Emma pulling back the curtains.

Avery shot up in her bed, fumbling for her pistol, which had slid between the mattress and the headboard. "How on earth did you get in the room?"

Emma looked at her, puzzled. "Through the servant's door, as usual, my lady."

"Humph." She felt foolish as she looked at the unlocked tapestry door on the other side of the room. It led to a small walk-in wardrobe, which in turn had another small door leading to the servants' stairs. If Emma-Stabbing-Hetty had wanted to stab her in her sleep, she could have done so a hundred times over.

It was therefore reasonable to conclude that Emma was not a murderess. Besides, she had no evidence of Emma's sordid past. The girl had been nothing but conscientious and hardworking since she'd arrived. Avery felt a pang of guilt. She really needed to stop this irrational and shameful condemnation of her fellow humans.

"I am undoubtedly a fool," she said aloud, abandoning the pistol and scrambling out of bed.

"Shall I leave the washstand where it is, or shall I move it back, my lady?" Emma asked.

"You may move it. I was just experimenting with the arrangement of the furniture."

"Certainly, my lady." Emma did not as much as blink.

Avery readied herself and went down to the dining room, passing a young man in the hallway. The new footman, no doubt.

He turned out to be a pleasant young chap with light brown hair and a friendly face. Much to her disappointment, he did not look at all like a criminal.

He'd bestowed a beaming smile upon her and bowed. "I am Fred, at your service." He followed her and continued beaming as he looked about the drawing room.

"Fred." Avery narrowed her eyes. Nice lad, but why was he smiling at the silver candlesticks and expensive china in the cupboard?

Jerkins cleared his throat and Fred sprang to attention, more eager than a puppy who'd found a new master.

Jerkins immediately sent him off to buy paper and ink, and Fred looked so excited about this mundane task that it occurred to her that maybe, just maybe, he wasn't a scallywag after all.

OVER BREAKFAST, Avery was mulling over the last few days' events when Jerkins appeared, holding her manuscript in his gloved hands.

"Have you read it?" Her hand crawled over her heart, which was pounding a little faster than usual.

"I have indeed, my lady. May I congratulate you on an excellently written story." He placed the manuscript on the table.

"Well, it's not finished yet." Avery took the stack of paper. "In fact, the real story has barely begun."

"I enjoyed what I've read so far."

"And?" Avery probed. "Do you have any suggestions?" *Would you like to tell me how a real highway robbery is carried out?* She bit her tongue before blurting out the words.

"Well..." He hemmed and hawed.

"Spit it out, Jerkins. I just want the truth." Avery braced herself.

"If you'll forgive me, there's just one tiny detail that seems a little irregular."

"A detail?" A frown appeared on her brow. "What do you mean?"

"It's the highland moors, my lady."

"Yes?" she pressed.

"Have you ever seen them?"

"Not really." Apart from Penmaron and London, she had not had the opportunity to travel at all.

"You see, it is impossible for a stallion to gallop across the Scottish moors at night."

"Is it?" Avery stared at him, thunderstruck.

"The moors are made of heather and peat, and if a

horse were to gallop across them, it would sink into the peat and stumble and likely end up breaking its legs."

"Oh."

"Unless, of course, there was a footpath he could ride on. But even then, it wouldn't be a straight road, but a narrow, winding path with stones and roots and ups and downs. Rather difficult to gallop at full speed."

"So, it would have to be a highway?"

"If you need it to gallop, then yes."

"Dash it, Jerkins. You just ruined my story." Avery pouted.

"I'm terribly sorry, my lady. Couldn't you move the setting to the lowlands?"

"It's not nearly as romantic as the highlands."

"I suppose not."

"Jerkins." Avery narrowed her eyes. "You seem to know a great deal about riding and the highland moors. Why is that?"

"I was born in the highlands, my lady." He smiled.

"You're a Scot!" Avery blurted out. That would, of course, explain the slight burr he had, in the way he rolled his 'r's. Why hadn't she noticed that before?

"I spent my first few years in Scotland before we moved south."

Avery looked at him curiously. Picturing little Jerkins toddling across the highland moors was a strangely appealing image.

"I may not be able to make it to the ball after all, my lady," he said suddenly. "I have not found a dancing master who can teach me to dance; and obtaining a voucher is proving to be an impossibility."

Avery had completely forgotten that she'd insisted he escort her to the ball.

She felt a pang of disappointment, then relief.

"That's all right, Jerkins." In fact, it was probably for the best. She found the idea of dancing with Jerkins, the highwayman, most unsettling. Only now she would have no one to dance with, and she braced herself for another flat evening where she would have to watch others dance.

Avery told herself she needed to be on her guard and never forget his true past.

By LATE AFTERNOON, Avery was getting ready for the ball. The red Persian gown was a la mode, and Emma had somehow managed to coax her stubbornly straight hair into curls.

"Where did you learn to do hair like that, Emma?" Avery pulled on a silver corkscrew curl and watched in fascination as it bounced back. Emma had skilfully worked several rosebuds into her hair, arranging them into a half-circle. She'd also plucked her eyebrows into two delicate arches, as Lady Jersey had suggested.

"I learnt from a French hairdresser during my time with the Duchess of Thistlethorpe, my lady."

Not a murderess from the rookery, then. She could not imagine 'Stabbing Hetty' ever learning how to arrange hair in such an elegant manner.

Though...the Duchess of Thistlethorpe?

"Never heard of her," Avery murmured.

"You wouldn't, my lady. Her Grace was rarely seen in society and led a very reclusive life."

Avery made a mental note to check *Debrett's Peerage* afterwards to see if she could find the name Thistlethorpe.

"I've always meant to ask, Emma," Avery said as she plucked a stray petal from her temple, "did Jerkins hire you through an agency?"

She looked at Emma in the mirror. The girl's hand froze above Avery's head for a second, then busied itself with straightening a flower.

"No, my lady. I was recommended by word of mouth." Emma dropped her hands and began tidying the dressing table. Then she turned to Avery and put her hands on her hips. "I must say, your ladyship looks magnificent tonight! You will be the belle of the ball."

Avery looked in the mirror as if she was seeing herself for the first time and found herself tearing up. For the first time in her life, she looked beautiful. "Thank you, Emma," she whispered.

She stood up, picked up her pen, and made a satisfyingly thick line through point four on her Never List.

As she waited for Belinda to arrive, Emma draped a dark blue cloak over her shoulders.

To her disappointment, her delinquent butler was nowhere in sight. Would his lips have curled into an appreciative smile at the sight of her in her red dress?

Avery's stomach roiled like goat's milk in a butter churn. She would never know, as Belinda ushered her out the door and into the carriage.

To Almack's they would go.

Chapter Fifteen

AVERY WASN'T QUITE SURE WHAT SHE'D EXPECTED— maybe for Almack's powerful doorkeeper to look down upon them disdainfully with flared nostrils as he held Belinda's forged ticket between his gloved fingers, and to publicly expose and ban them from entering the hallowed grounds, so that they'd have to slink home with heads hanging, forevermore shamed.

It came as something of a surprise when Belinda greeted the doorkeeper with a cheerful, "Good evening, Winston," as she handed him her ticket.

He merely threw a cursory glance at it and replied with an affable smile, "Welcome back to Almack's, Mrs Wimplethorpe," and opened the door for her.

He nodded as Avery handed him her ticket. "Welcome, Lady Avery. I trust you will enjoy yourself this evening."

He ushered them inside, where the butler was waiting to take their coats.

"How many times have you been to Almack's?" Avery

asked Belinda, once she'd digested the fact that Belinda's ticket hadn't been forged and that they'd been admitted to the temple of the *haut ton* without so much as a blink.

"This is only the second time this Season. I used to attend frequently with Freddie, of course."

"Of course," Avery echoed. She could not quite explain why she had the nagging feeling that this Freddie might never have existed.

Almack's ballroom was framed by gilded columns and mirrors. Pale blue damask curtains hung from the floor-to-ceiling windows, and the orchestra played from a trellised balcony. The place was modestly decorated with green ivy, and red ropes divided the room for the dancers.

There were not quite as many people as had been at the public charity ball last week.

A lady separated from a group to their left and floated towards them. "Ah, there you are. I wondered when you'd appear."

Avery looked into Lady Jersey's twinkling black eyes.

"And I see you've taken my advice regarding your dress. Well done. As you can see, I have grown quite fond of my new headdress."

Avery recognised it as the one she'd sewn.

"It has become quite the rage, and I am pleased." The feather bobbed with every movement of her head.

"My lady," Avery stammered. "I must thank you for graciously granting me a voucher. I would never have dreamed of applying for one. I am very grateful to be here."

Lady Jersey waved her fan away. "Nonsense, of course you should be here. It promises to be a most amusing evening." To Avery's surprise, she turned and gave Belinda a cool nod. "Mrs Wimplethorpe, how do you do?"

Belinda nodded back just as grandly.

"Mrs Wimplethorpe is my cousin," Avery felt the need to explain.

"Indeed? But I am not surprised. Mrs Wimplethorpe is one of those prodigious creatures who seems to be related to half the people in this room." She gave Belinda a slightly sour smile. "Do enjoy yourselves, ladies, even though it looks like the gentlemen are as of yet few and far between. I see I must go and rescue Lord Billingswhile, who is being cornered by three overly ambitious matrons. He cannot be monopolised by these matchmakers so early in the evening. We need him for at least four more dances."

With a nod, she floated away.

Belinda's bright smile faded after she was gone. "I vow, Cousin, I do not like her. She has a sharp tongue to the point of being ill-bred. But she seems to have developed a liking for you, and that is good. She is a powerful ally to have." She took Avery's arm. "Come, let's see if we can find some more acquaintances. I think I see Colonel Sullivan under the balcony."

"Who is Colonel Sullivan?"

"You don't know Colonel Sullivan? My dear! We are related through Aunt Hannah, of course."

"Of course." Avery had no idea who Aunt Hannah was. She allowed herself to be dragged across the ballroom to be introduced to a portly but genial-looking gentleman with whiskers. When the music began to play a cheerful Scottish country dance, he immediately asked Belinda to dance.

She agreed, and he led her to take their place in the set.

Once again, Avery found herself alone in the middle of a London ballroom, feeling rather foolish.

She could do one of two things: sit in the dreaded chairs by the wall again, doing the name "wallflower" honour, or attempt to entertain herself despite it all. Without Belinda.

Since dancing was not to be, Avery decided to seek out the tearoom. For if she could not dance, she would eat.

THEY WERE CERTAINLY right in what they were saying about the food, Avery thought as she bit into a cake that was drier than Sahara dust. The crumbs stuck to the roof of her mouth and were difficult to swallow. She grabbed a glass of lemonade and drank thirstily. She had never tasted anything so revolting. It tasted like water with a drop of vinegar in it. The orgeat was no better; it tasted like slightly sugared water. And she would pass on the ratafia; surely that syrupy brownish-red liquid had been scooped from a puddle in St James's Park.

"Here you are." Belinda appeared breathless and with two spots of red on her cheeks. On her arm was the colonel, who was breathing equally heavily from the exertion of having danced the Scottish reel. "I'm awfully thirsty from all that dancing!"

"I'm afraid they only have lemonade or orgeat, Mrs

Wimplethorpe." The colonel handed her a glass. "I advise you to pass on the ratafia. The lemonade is dreadful stuff, but better than nothing." He drank an entire glass of the ghastly stuff himself in one gulp. "I'll go and procure us some food."

"I'll ask the colonel to dance with you, if it doesn't occur to him to ask you next," Belinda whispered in her ear as the man left to fetch some of the Sahara cake.

"Oh, please don't." Avery felt thoroughly humiliated. "If it doesn't occur to him to ask me on his own initiative, I'd rather you didn't trouble him about it."

"It's no trouble at all," Belinda argued. "But where has he gone now? Vexatious man."

Colonel Sullivan seemed to have fallen into the clutches of a woman who was clearly trying to set him up with her daughter, a pale debutante standing beside her.

"Leave him alone," Avery said wearily, turning back to her plate. She took a slice of thin bread, buttered it, and ate that instead. The bread was stale, and the butter wasn't fresh either, she concluded.

Just then, a tall gentleman entered. He paused at the door and let his eyes wander lazily around the room with an air of infinite boredom.

He was dressed according to the latest fashion, in an exquisitely tailored black tailcoat and breeches that were moulded to his form, revealing broad shoulders and powerful thighs. He had thick, black, windswept hair that was slightly long and curled at the nape of his neck. He had a clean-cut jaw and a proud patrician nose on a face that was more striking than handsome, a contemptuous, wintry smile playing around his lips. He exuded the kind of toplofty boredom that only an aristocrat extremely high in the instep was capable of.

Avery had grown very still. A piece of bread may have fallen out of her open mouth.

"Dear sweet heavens, who is he?" Belinda breathed beside her.

A hush had fallen over the room as his appearance was noted. Then a low hum commenced as the whispers and murmurs began.

Unimpressed by the general commotion his appearance seemed to have caused, the gentleman raised his quizzing glass, surveyed the room, and then strolled towards the card room.

"Who is he?" More than one person whispered.

"Stap my vitals, if it isn't—Blackshurst! The devil." A gentleman in a Prussian blue coat approached him. "Since when are you in the country? Saw you in Paris last. You disappear from the face of this earth and suddenly you just stroll into Almack's?"

The man stared at him haughtily, and at first it looked as if he was about to give him a direct cut. Then an amused smile stole onto his face, transforming it entirely. It was breathtaking to watch.

"Ashburn. You have grown old, man," he drawled.

Two more men joined them, and there was a general round of hand shaking and shoulder slapping, then they all disappeared into the card room.

"I say, that was interesting," Belinda said. "Did you see him? So...so manly. Handsome is not the right word. But striking. Definitely striking. There is an aura of danger about him that I find quite attractive. Avery? Are you quite well?"

Avery had frozen into a statue.

"Oh, I daresay you're not the only woman who's been smitten and left speechless. Ashburn called him Blackshurst," Belinda mused. "The name is familiar. I wonder when I heard it—oh! Oh!" She put her hand to her mouth as her eyes grew round. "Not that Blackshurst, surely?"

"Yes." Avery had finally found her voice. She cleared her throat as it came out all raspy and hoarse. "That Blackshurst, alas. My landlord. Or rather, my brother's. That is, my brother rented his townhouse from him. I thought he was abroad. He must have returned early. How awkward."

"You don't say! I had no idea he was your landlord. I am quite shocked." Her eyes widened in horror.

Avery shook her head in confusion. "It's certainly an inconvenience, but nothing to be shocked about."

"But Avery, don't you know? The newspapers were full of him! Mind you, it was years and years ago, but still. Blackshurst is known to be a terrible rakehell, possibly the worst there ever was." Belinda leaned forward to whisper. "He's known as the Black Earl!"

Avery felt quite sick to her stomach and it wasn't because she'd had too much lemonade. "Really? That sounds rather melodramatic. He can't be that bad, can he?"

"Haven't you heard the stories?"

"Pray, enlighten me, Cousin."

"Blackshurst has the reputation of being a womaniser

par excellence. He is quite depraved. They say he has ruined several debutantes in this very room just by looking at them. When Blackshurst is on the prowl, no woman is safe, I tell you, no one!" Belinda seemed curiously excited by this. "The number of duels he's fought is countless, and he's a legendary, deadly shot. It is a mystery to me why he is here, as the patronesses should have revoked his voucher long ago. We make it all too easy for him, foolish women that we are. Look, there is Princess Esterhazy, all agog to get him out of the card room. Although, of course, she may have once been one of his paramours. Of course! So that is why he has a voucher. He must have seduced at least one, if not all, of the patronesses to get his way."

The two women watched as the Princess walked arm in arm with Lady Jersey into the ballroom, fluttering with excitement and giggling like a pair of girls who'd just left the school room.

Avery shook her head in amazement.

Her fingers were sticky. When she looked down, she realised she'd clamped her fingers around a last piece of seed cake and squashed it to a pulp. She dropped it onto her plate.

"Let's return to the ballroom, Belinda." She wiped her fingers on a napkin.

"But don't you want to see if the Princess and Lady Jersey succeed in luring him out of the card room?"

"No. It is better to stay out of his way. I'd rather not cross paths with him," said Avery. "Let's get back to the ballroom and disappear into the crowd there."

Belinda patted her arm. "Never fear, Cousin. If he

evicts you from the house, you can stay with me at Portland Place. It would be a pleasure to have you."

Avery felt touched. "Thank you, Belinda, that is truly kind of you. But let us hope it won't come to that."

"Oh! Over there is Lady Winworth. I must introduce you." Belinda dragged her across the room and introduced her to a small, stout lady with cheerful eyes and her brother, Lord Gerington, who wore his ginger hair toupeed high above his head. Avery thought he looked absurd, but he made up for it with his affability towards her.

"A dance?" he said, and Avery perked up.

Finally!

He bowed—in the direction of Belinda, who replied, "Oh! But my cousin here is an excellent dancer and will certainly enjoy dancing the next set with you!"

Lord Gerington gave Avery an apologetic smile. "Indeed! The next set will be yours, Lady Avery. But I would be honoured if you would grace the ballroom floor with me this time, Mrs Wimplethorpe."

"Oh, go and dance," Avery said good-naturedly.

Belinda shot Avery a contrite look as she took his arm as he led them to their positions for the next set.

Belinda danced gracefully, her eyes sparkling with joy as Lord Gerington led her in a turn around him.

"What a beautiful couple!" Lady Winworth beamed. "Don't you think? Widows, both. Same age. You'd think they'd make an excellent match. Except neither has a farthing to fly with." She fanned herself as she sighed. "I don't see a future here."

Avery felt affronted on behalf of her cousin. "Belinda

is young, beautiful and has a lovely personality. One would think that this is where the true value of a person lies, not how full the coffers are."

The woman snapped her fan shut. "I see you take offence at my words. Indeed, you misunderstand; I do not mean that Mrs Wimplethorpe is not an excellent match for George, but the other way round." She leaned forward and whispered, "He plays, you see."

"Oh."

"Indeed." She patted Avery's arm and walked away.

She sighed as she watched the dancing couples.

Once again, she was alone in the middle of a ball.

Avery was getting tired of it all. The dance would last a good half an hour, so she might as well sit down while she waited for Belinda and Lord Gerington to finish.

With a resigned sigh, she sat down in her seat of shame by the wall and waited.

Who would have thought that balls would be so boring? The only excitement had been Blackshurst's appearance, but then he'd taken himself off to the card room. There was otherwise nothing interesting happening here. She'd be better off spending her time at home, finishing her stories. Regretting that she did not have a pen and paper with her to write on, Avery started writing in her head to pass the time.

Her highwayman was about to rob a coach containing his love interest. Of course, he would have to kidnap her. But how? As Avery pondered on the conundrum of whether he should do so with a pistol or a sword, a shadow fell over her.

"Lady Avery. I believe this is my dance," a deep, commanding voice said above her.

Her gaze travelled up a pair of long legs in black satin breeches, to a silver-striped waistcoat, followed by a snowy starched cravat, intricately tied in the latest fashion. She tilted her neck backwards to take in his black coat stretching over erect shoulders.

Avery's heart made a funny lurch, then hammered away at rapid speed.

One hand was extended. Waiting.

Eyes hard as steel met hers in a steady gaze.

When had the ballroom become so excessively warm?

Why did she not have a fan?

"I..." And what on earth did one say in a situation like this? *I'd love to dance, but not with you,* seemed awkward. *I'd rather not because I'm afraid of you* was even worse. Maybe the correct thing would be to say, *We were not introduced,* and then to simply ignore him. How dare he have the audacity to ask her to dance without an introduction?

Perhaps there was no need to say anything at all, for Lord Blackshurst simply took her hand in his and, with a gentle tug, pulled her from the chair and led her to the dance floor. Avery obeyed like a skittish lamb being herded by its sheepdog.

The orchestra began to play the wistful three-four time of a waltz.

"A waltz! 'Twas about time!" There was a general murmur in the room.

He pulled her into his arms, and she found herself

staring at the diamond studs of his waistcoat. Impossibly close, indecently close, she could feel his warm breath brushing her temple and the scent of his seductive cologne of bay rum, bergamot, and citron entering her nostrils.

Then he led her into a turn.

They danced.

Neither of them spoke. The ballroom blurred around them as they twirled and twirled, all sense of time and place lost. He guided her skillfully with a gentle pressure on her waist. Nervous at first that she would trample on his feet, Avery threw all her reservations to the wind, threw her head back and savoured the sensation of being held in strong arms, simply dancing on a cloud, on light feet, carried away by the music.

This!

This was all she'd ever wanted.

Her lips parted in a happy smile.

All too soon the music ended, the dance slowed, and yet he did not release her, but held her a little closer, pressing her to his chest.

Both their breaths heaved.

He lifted his hand to lift her chin.

There was a disquieting glint in his eyes, and her own felt moist.

"Thank you." Her lips parted. "That was beautiful beyond words."

He lifted his hand and gently wiped away a tear that had crept from the corner of one eye. His finger was warm.

She shivered as his touch sizzled from her cheek to

the tip of her toes, his gaze holding her spellbound, his lips impossibly close.

Her whole body burned.

She shook her head involuntarily.

He dropped his hand.

"We must return," she said abruptly, killing the moment. "My cousin will be wondering where I am."

Avery took his arm and led him away from the dance floor.

However, she did not lead him to the seat where Belinda was waiting with Lady Winworth, but out the door. She dragged him across the foyer, between the marble columns that formed shadowy nooks and crannies, behind which were mysterious doors leading to the servants' stairs, the wardrobe, and smaller rooms.

A couple emerged giggling from one of these rooms.

Avery steered him towards them.

"A love nook?" Blackshurst muttered as Avery pushed him inside. "Is that wise?"

It was a small, almost wardrobe-sized room used as storage space. Avery put her hands on her hips and faced him.

"Plague and pestilence, Jerkins. What in blazes was that all about?"

Chapter Sixteen

JERKINS-CUM-BLACKSHURST RAISED A SARDONIC EYEBROW. "Having a tête-á-tête with a lady?" His eyes trailed down her body. "With a most charming lady, indeed. In a most interesting place." He lifted her hand, slowly peeled off her glove and placed a series of light butterfly kisses on the inside of her wrist.

Her whole body went up in flames. She would end up in a pile of ashes at his feet if he did not stop this immediately.

Her tirade turned into a stuttering, mangled mess of words.

She pulled her arm away, but she could still feel his lips on her tingling skin.

"Stop this immediately. Jerkins, have you completely lost your mind?"

He seemed unperturbed as he pulled his mouth into a lopsided smile. "Isn't this what you wanted? I do not understand why you are so upset."

"They will discover who you are latest when the real

Blackshurst returns! It will be a scandal beyond anything the *ton* has ever known, and it will blow up in our faces with a bang louder than Guy Fawkes's explosion under Parliament. Then both of us will be clapped into Bedlam." Avery wrung her hands. "Why did you have to choose to impersonate Blackshurst, of all people?" She groaned.

"Lady Avery. Has anyone ever told you that your eyes flash the most enchanting green when you are angry?" He gave her a smile. "You are a delight."

Jerkins was clearly unwilling to step out of character. She threw up both hands with a groan.

"Very well. I see there is no reasoning with you. Perhaps it is best if you remain in your role. Go and do what this Blackshurst does best, lest anyone discover you are not the real Blackshurst. You must stay in character and seduce someone!" She waved her hand at him.

"I am in the process of doing just that," he murmured, "except that the lady in question seems sadly oblivious to my efforts. Alas, I seem to have lost my touch."

Avery spluttered.

He gave her a devilish smile, reached out, and brushed his hand lightly across her cheek. He leaned down, his mouth approaching hers.

Avery stilled.

Then he reached behind her for the door latch, a slightly regretful smile playing about his lips.

The noise of the rest of the world reached them, the strains of music, the chatter.

Blackshurst bowed. "After you, my lady."

Avery stepped out. "It was a lovely waltz, wasn't it—" she turned to Blackshurst.

She blinked.

Where had he gone?

And. Good heavens. Had he really been about to kiss her?

Had she imagined it all?

It was excruciatingly hot. She fanned herself with her glove and looked around for Belinda.

"Avery!" A woman's voice said behind her.

She whirled around to find Lady Jersey descending on her.

"I must say, you and Blackshurst have managed to become the talk of the evening!" Her dark eyes twinkled merrily, as if this amused her to no end. "I had no idea you were so, er, intimately acquainted."

"Neither did I," Avery murmured. "I mean, indirectly. He's my brother's landlord."

"Ah, of course! How exciting! You do know he is one of the most sought-after bachelors here tonight, despite his, shall we say, rather colourful past?" She waved a gloved hand. "I would not have given him a voucher in the first place if I did not believe that half the stories told about him are exaggerations. The *ton* loves to wag its tongue and create scandal where there is none. But much time has passed since then, and I think we have all grown older and wiser. Including Blackshurst." Her forehead wrinkled into a frown. "People do change, don't they? I must say, I hardly recognised him, he looks so different now. But it was all so long ago, and I was barely out myself when he made the papers."

"Indeed." The knot in Avery's stomach tightened again. When would she, or anyone else, realise that Blackshurst was not who he said he was? What happened to impostors? Were they beheaded and thrown into the Tower? The order of things was negotiable.

"But look at you! You danced with him!" Lady Jersey beamed at her.

"Yes." Avery cleared her throat. "It was very nice."

"We all watched with breathless fascination. You dance well. The waltz is quite romantic, don't you think? Even if it does have a reputation for being somewhat improper. I have always said we have to move with the times and finally allow dancing at Almack's. Oh, look. Here is Lord Grantham."

A handsome dandy approached them, bowed to Lady Jersey, and asked to be introduced to Avery.

"It would be my greatest pleasure, Lady Avery, if you would do me the honour of standing with me for the next set."

"What an excellent idea. Go and dance, children," Lady Jersey said benevolently.

Avery pretended to look at her dance card, which was empty, and nodded.

Thus, it came that Avery was able to dance not only one, but four more sets, as now the gentlemen scrambled to be introduced to her, and she had no lack of dancing partners.

"It was incredible," she told Belinda on their way

home. It was well past midnight, and her feet were sore from all the dancing.

"I'm so happy for you," Belinda gushed. "And look how they were all over you, the gentlemen. Right after Blackshurst danced with you." Belinda shook her head, her curls bouncing. "Really, Avery! When I saw you dancing with him, I almost fainted. And the waltz too! The whole ballroom was watching. He was so flirtatious with you."

Avery put her hands on her heated cheeks. "We were just dancing. We barely exchanged two words."

Belinda shook her head. "You weren't just dancing. It looked like he was making love to you in the middle of the dance floor. It was very improper, though I daresay one can't expect anything less from Blackshurst. A moment longer, and they would have thrown you out."

"Oh dear." If she only knew. Avery felt ice-cold heat coursing through her veins every time she thought of his warm lips on the inside of her wrist. She rubbed the tingling skin.

"Very well done by Jerkins, wouldn't you say? He should remain Blackshurst all the time. Suits him so much better than the butler role." Belinda leaned back with a yawn.

Avery sat up straight. "You knew that he was Jerkins all along?"

"Naturally." She winked. "I wasn't born yesterday. Clever ruse, to get him to dance with you. It worked very well, did it not?"

"It—it did," Avery stuttered.

"No need to look so concerned. I will not breathe a

word about it to anyone, I promise. We are family, after all, and need to mind each other's secrets. You look rather flushed, Cousin," Belinda observed. "No doubt from dancing all night, but I must say it suits you. We must make sure you dance more! With Blackshurst." She grinned.

Avery perked up. "I've danced through the night!" she said in amazement. "I really did!"

One of the biggest items on her list had been accomplished.

Chapter Seventeen

THE NEXT MORNING, AVERY SLEPT LONG AND WAS woken by Emma bringing in a tray of hot chocolate and a croissant. She ate breakfast in bed, feeling like a queen. She picked up *Town and Country Magazine*, which lay next to her cup of hot chocolate, and turned to the featured Tête-à-Tête article.

Ladies beware, the Black Earl has returned from Paris and has been spotted at Almack's.
He is as big a scoundrel as ever and has set many a woman's heart aflutter. For those who may not remember, the Black Earl is famous for having seduced no less than one hundred and fifty-four ladies, women, and damsels, although some would put the number higher at two hundred and thirty-four.

Avery snorted.

After fleecing Colonel R of half his fortune in the card

*room, he was seen waltzing with Lady AH, a highly inap-
propriate dance that has only recently been sanctioned by
the patronesses...*

She choked on her hot chocolate. For the first time in
her life, she'd waltzed at a ball and promptly made the
scandal sheets. That was quite an achievement.

She rubbed her wrist. Her cheeks heated at the
memory of his lips touching her skin. How could she ever
look Jerkins in the eye after last night?

Jerkins—the highwayman who'd risen from the dead,
posing as a butler who impersonated a lord. And not just
any lord, but a rakehell.

Avery groaned. This could not, would not, end well.

She stood up and pulled on the bell.

"Help me get ready, Emma, and tell Jerkins I need to
speak to him immediately."

"Yes, my lady. I believe he is already waiting for you
in the drawing room."

Then, of course, there was the matter of Stabbing
Hetty and the Scallywag Footman.

Not to mention the Counterfeit Cousin.

Who was next? The Nefarious Cook? The Villainous
Coachman?

Avery dressed and went to the drawing room, her
heart galloping faster than a racehorse, but Jerkins was
not there.

She crossed the hallway to go to the study and found
Fred the footman waiting there, still gazing happily at the
expensive china displayed in the vitrine.

"Where's Jerkins?" she snapped, and immediately

regretted her tone. She usually treated her domestic servants with courtesy and always made sure never to let her ill temper out on them. It wasn't Fred's fault that Jerkins had made such a dashing lord who'd set her heart to flutter last night.

"I shall fetch him anon." Fred smiled at her, and she grumpily concluded that he smiled altogether too much. It was suspicious.

She sat at the desk in the study, practising the words she would tell her miscreant butler. The most reasonable thing to do, no doubt, was to dismiss him. But Avery could not gather up the courage to do so. Dismissing someone was no easy feat, as she'd had no practice whatsoever doing so. Besides, it had been her idea, initially, to ask Jerkins to go to the ball. It would be hardly fair if she dismissed him for that.

She got up and went to the window, pulling the curtain aside to look out onto the wet street.

She would have to tell him that, even though it had been her idea, initially, it was not the thing at all for him to be parading about as Blackshurst, for what would they do if the man ever returned for real? Then there would be two Blackshursts. Or, worse still, someone would recognise him as Lord Fothergill's butler and unmask him. She would thank him for a lovely dance last night and then tell him never, ever to assume the role of Blackshurst again.

"Good morning, my lady. I trust you enjoyed the ball last night." His gravelly voice suddenly sounded behind her.

Avery jumped.

"Good heavens, Jerkins, you gave me a fright. Don't sneak up on me like a thief in the night." She put a hand over her pounding heart.

Jerkins was wearing his usual dark, baggy suit, and his grey wig. The wig added twenty years to his age. She'd always assumed the hideous grey thing hid a bald head, not a head full of glorious long, thick black hair curling up at the back of his neck. And why was he stooping when she knew he could walk straight as a lamppost? And waltz like a god, despite his initial protestations to the contrary. Although now, in the light of day, she couldn't for the life of her imagine she had ever danced with him. Any hint that he had ever assumed the identity of Blackshurst was completely gone.

What a gifted actor he was!

"I apologise for startling you, my lady. I bear some bad news. There was an unfortunate incident last night while you were at the ball. I am afraid that robbers entered the house last night."

"What! Has the house been robbed?" Her eyes fell on Tom's gun cabinet, but it seemed untouched.

"We are still investigating the matter, in addition to listing the missing items. However, the damage does not appear to be extensive, and apart from two missing silver spoons, which I suspect have been misplaced, there appear to be only random items missing from below stairs."

Avery's hand went to her throat. "What happened?"

He clasped his hands behind his back as he reported. "The thief forced his way through the kitchen door leading to the garden. The lock is broken. He rummaged about below the stairs, setting everything in disarray. This included the cook's bedroom, the pantry, and my own room. The cook had the day off and spent the night with her family. It seems the thief never ventured upstairs, and Emma, Fred, Mary, and Cilly have their bedrooms in the attic, so they were unaware of what was happening downstairs."

"Who are Mary and Cilly?"

"The house maid and the scullery maid." He raised an eyebrow.

"Ah." She'd seen a pointy-faced creature scurrying about the corridors the other day. That must have been Cilly, no doubt. She wondered if Jerkins had hired her from the rookery as well.

It was on the tip of Avery's tongue to say that maybe it wasn't a burglary at all, maybe the thief was in the house. A criminal from St Giles. Or a former highwayman.

She shook herself. This was nonsense. Jerkins had an alibi, and Fred couldn't have been stupid enough to burgle the house on the very day he was hired.

Could he?

"Needless to say, the runners have been informed and a new lock has already been installed. Fred will now sleep under the stairs and guard the kitchen door—with a pistol. Have no doubt, my lady, the thief will be apprehended. I will personally see to it that you are safe in this house and that not a hair on your head will ever be harmed." There was something fierce, almost savage, in his face as he said this.

Avery shivered. "I wonder what they were looking for?"

"It is an enigma, my lady, since there is nothing of value kept below stairs."

"Well, perhaps they heard Tom and his family had left and thought they would have an easy time emptying the house, only to find that was not the case," she surmised. "Something must have scared him off."

"It's possible. The fact is that someone must have been watching the house, aware of our comings and goings. Someone followed you back from your trip to the rookery. That is no coincidence. I must insist that you are cautious and only go out when necessary, and only then accompanied by Fred or myself."

Avery, of course, had no intention of doing so. She decided to leave Jerkins in the belief that she was submitting to his demands. The best way to go about doing so was to change the topic.

She showed him the article in the *Town and Country Magazine*.

"About last night. I have no idea how you managed to get into Almack's, Jerkins. Did you bribe them? Did you forge the voucher? No, don't tell me, I'd rather not know. But your appearance is causing a stir, and you'll have to be careful not to be exposed. So far, the *ton* seems to be swallowing your version of Blackshurst, and you are doing a very good job of playing the aristocrat with the haughty composure. But I have a feeling that this cannot —will not—go well for long."

He skimmed the article, then folded it. "Blackshurst is a scoundrel, but there is no need to be overly concerned for his safety. There is, however, every reason to be wary of his rakish tendencies."

Avery choked. Really, Jerkins was too absurd! He was warning her about himself while posing as a notorious rake?

"Pray, do not worry, Jerkins. I do not intend to become number two hundred and thirty-five."

The corner of his mouth twitched.

He bowed and turned to leave.

"One more thing, Jerkins. A rather important question, if you would please answer it honestly."

"Your ladyship?" He looked at her expectantly.

She took a sharp intake of breath. "Are you, perchance, Jax Tyrrell?"

Chapter Eighteen

A FLICKER OF SURPRISE DANCED ACROSS HIS EYES before he hooded them. "I am not, my lady. Jax Tyrrell was sent to the gallows more than two decades ago."

"Are you certain?"

"What makes you think otherwise?"

She tugged at her lower lip. She didn't want to tell him about the notebook and the poetry book she'd found. Not yet. On the other hand, she needed to give him a reason for her suspicion.

"I saw you that day in St Giles," she finally confessed.

There was an unsettling glint in his eyes. "You seem to be making a habit of visiting the rookery. That must stop."

She plaited her muslin dress between her fingers. "Let us not repeat this discussion. I must insist on an answer."

"As I have explained, it is rather difficult to find suitable retainers at present, and I have had to resort to unorthodox methods to find people. Make no mistake, I

143

have thoroughly investigated their backgrounds and found them suitable."

"But if you picked them up from the rookery, how can you tell they're not criminals?" Avery asked, her voice full of suspicion. "You won't allow me to visit the rookery, yet here you are bringing the rookery to my house. What if one of them was responsible for the burglary?"

Jerkins stared at her for a few long moments. "A person's lowly upbringing doesn't automatically make them a lawbreaker," he reprimanded her.

"Of course not." She bit on her lip.

"I have found Fred, Emma, Cilly, and Mary to be trustworthy. That's all I need." His dark gaze was intense. "What is also necessary is that you trust me. Unconditionally."

"I trust you." Her voice was slightly uneven. She trusted him about as much as a mouse trusted a hawk.

"That's good, then," Jerkins said quietly.

Really, she needed to regain control of the situation. She was the mistress; he was her servant. She had to tell him what to do, not the other way round.

Avery cleared her throat. "Well, that's done then, Jerkins. I have much to do. Call me a carriage, please."

He did not move. "Where do you intend to go, my lady?"

She waved her hand. "To Hounslow Heath. I have some research to do."

"Very well, my lady. As Fred is out on an errand and Mrs Wimplethorpe is still sleeping, I shall accompany you."

JERKINS SAT across from her in the carriage. Just before he got in, Avery noticed that he'd tucked a pistol into his coat.

"I thought you didn't use pistols," she said sweetly. "You don't condone violence."

"Well, my lady," he threw her a brilliant smile, "it appears I lied."

His unexpected admission threw her into confusion. Then she scowled. "You played me the fool when I tried to shoot the cherry tree, and you pretended not to know the difference between a flintlock's barrel and the hilt." She wondered what else he'd lied about. "You also told a bouncer about not being able to dance."

"Tell me what other things you have on your list that we need to accomplish," he replied instead.

"We?" She raised an eyebrow.

"We." He sat back and crossed his arms.

Avery narrowed her eyes. A mischievous thought flashed through her. If he intended to follow her like a shadow, she would make it as difficult as possible. She leaned back in anticipation. "You've seen my list, so don't pretend you don't know. But I may have to change some of the things on it."

"Very well. Such as?"

She tapped a gloved finger against her lips. "I must, of course, visit the haberdasher for more ribbons, the milliner for a new bonnet, the shoemaker for a new pair of boots, and the dressmaker for a new fitting. The old dress is a little too long." She'd had enough of modistes, but she would not mind visiting Madame Minion again, only to see Jerkins kicking his boots in the dust for hours, waiting for her while she took her time getting fitted for her gown.

Jerkins's face fell, but he nodded.

Avery suppressed a smile.

"I must, of course, visit the Temple of the Muses for some new books, the Egyptian Hall, Sir Hans Sloane's collection at the British Museum, an art exhibition at the Royal Academy, the menagerie at the Tower, Covent Garden Theatre—I must see Kean!—Don Giovanni at the Opera, and of course Astley's Amphitheatre, and oh! A travelling peep show and the Fireproof Lady at Bartholomew Fair." She ticked each off on her fingers.

Jerkins looked overwhelmed.

"And a boxing match and a gambling den," she added quickly. She had no interest whatsoever in seeing either of them.

"Certainly not," he said promptly, glaring at her.

"Certainly yes. It is much needed research. It would be very valuable for me to see a live duel as well; don't you think that could be done at the early morning house in Hyde Park or Regent's Park? It would be very helpful to see a person get shot and die, for the authenticity of my writing, of course. On the subject of death, it might be instructive to be a witness to a public hanging. Nothing is more annoying than an inauthentically written death scene. Oh! Do you think one might get a look at some corpses in the anatomy school?"

Jerkins choked.

Satisfied that she had rendered him entirely speech-less, she blithely continued, "So you see, I—or, as you insist, we—shall be quite busy the next few days. But look, we have already arrived at the Heath." She looked outside. "Tell the coachman to look for Jax Tyrrell's gravestone, if you please." She folded her hands in her lap.

Jerkins stared at her for a moment before finding his words. "I've never met a woman who takes as much pleasure in gory and morbid subjects as you do."

"Thank you, Jerkins, that is a wonderful compliment. Now, let us examine Jax Tyrrell's grave."

It was a rough-hewn grey slab of stone amid low shrubbery, easily overlooked.

Here lies Jax Tyrrell
The Notorious Highwayman
Executed at Tyburn 7th November 1790.

AVERY TOOK out her notebook and made some notes.

"Hm. Somewhat of a let-down, to be honest. One would have thought the fellow would have received at least a poem inscribed onto his gravestone, on account of his legendary status. What a shame I did not think of bringing a flower to leave on his grave, but I suppose that would not have been seemly, him having been a dastardly criminal and all that. What do you think?"

A gust of wind blew across the heath and tugged at Jerkins's wig. He did not answer, but stood motionless, staring at the gravestone with a grim set of the jaw, his hands in his pockets, his shoulders hunched.

"Jerkins?"

Avery had to call twice more.

Jerkins looked up abruptly.

"Are you quite well?" Avery tilted her head to study him. Was she imagining it, or was he a shade paler around the mouth than usual? Perhaps it was merely her imagination, for the clouds had obscured the sun and it was getting dark. A drop of rain splashed on her nose.

"I'm perfectly well. Are we done now? Excellent." He didn't wait for an answer but took her by the elbow and led her back into the carriage as the rain began to fall.

Avery continued to take notes in the carriage, looking up at him periodically through her lashes.

She put her pencil and notebook away and crossed her arms. "Tell me about your family, Jerkins."

"What do you want to know, my lady?"

"You said you spent your childhood in Scotland. Did you have siblings? How did you become a butler?"

After a short pause, he began to speak. "My story is unspectacular. My parents were crofters in the north. We lost our farm because of the clearances. My parents packed up and moved to the south, where my father was promised work. Instead, he died in a coach accident. My mother became ill and died soon after. I was taken in by a rich man who, for some inexplicable reason, took a liking to me and gave me a position in his household as a footman. I have been in service ever since. After he died, I was taken on by Blackshurst."

"I'm very sorry about your parents," Avery said quietly. "It can't have been an easy life."

Jerkins shrugged. "It is the unspectacular life of most of the commoners here."

"And Blackshurst? What was it like working for him?"

"He's a lord like any other. It makes no difference whether I work for him or your brother. They're all the same in the end."

"Is it true what the scandal sheets say about him?"

The shadow of a smile crossed his face. "About the two hundred and thirty-something women?"

"Yes."

He thought about it. "They got it wrong. I seem to have counted at least two hundred and sixty-four."

Avery shrieked.

Jerkins laughed, a deep, rolling laugh that made her pulse skitter alarmingly.

"You're bamming me," she said breathlessly.

"I might. A little." He leaned forward, his eyes gleaming behind his glasses. "My turn. Why this interest in criminals like Jax Tyrrell?"

"I told you, I'm attempting to write a story. You were the one who put the idea into my head in the first place, if I may remind you."

"Aye, and I'm beginning to regret it deeply. You romanticise criminals." He shook his head. "Did you obtain the information you needed?"

"I may have."

"Good. So, no more poking around filthy public houses, asking seedy people about Jax Tyrrell, eh?"

"For the time being, yes." She smiled brightly at Jerkins. "Will you read the next chapter of the story for me and give me written feedback?"

"It would be my pleasure, my lady," he replied.

Excellent. She would have another sample of his writing to compare with the notes in the poetry book.

BLACKSHURST SENT ROSES.

Daily.

Bouquets of plain scarlet roses tied only with lace, sometimes a whole basket of tiny white soapwort flowers and greenery. Each bouquet came with a simple, cream-coloured card, printed in bold black letters: Blackshurst.

No signature, no note, nothing.

Grantham had also sent a bouquet of violets, but these were completely overshadowed by Blackshurst's roses.

Jerkins carried the bouquets into her sitting room every morning with a straight face.

"Another bouquet from Blackshurst, my lady," he announced in a bored voice.

"Thank you. How very silly of him." She buried her face in the velvet rose petals to hide her burning cheeks.

Common sense also told her that Grantham's violets should be more cherished, that they might be from a serious suitor. But Avery found it hard to accept the idea of Grantham as her suitor. She'd only danced with him once and could barely remember his face.

Then again, she'd only danced once with Black-shurst, and they hadn't even spoken during the entire dance. If it hadn't been so absurd, Avery would have felt flattered; part of her would have wanted to indulge the illusion of being wooed by a powerful lord with whom she had danced and who was now courting her, and with whom she might—just might—have fallen a little in love.

But of course, it was all nonsense. It was all Jerkins. Jerkins who'd agreed to play a role all too well, so well in fact that she'd more than once found herself believing he was an entirely separate identity. She wondered where he'd obtained all those calling cards; then she remembered that, having worked as Blackshurst's butler, he'd had plenty of opportunity to collect his lordship's cards.

She wanted to dance with him again into the small hours, basking in the illusion of the romance of it all. Because, of course, it was all an illusion. Nothing more.

"Your MAIL, MY LADY." Jerkins handed her a tray of letters and invitations.

To Avery's delight, she'd received an invitation to a rout from Lady Jersey, an invitation to dinner from Lady Rathke, with whom she'd only had a few minutes' conversation, an invitation to a masquerade at Vauxhall, and a ridotto al Fresco from a Lady Mortimer, which Avery found intriguing. But for the life of her, she could not remember who the lady was.

"May I be so bold as to recommend that you accept Lady Jersey's invitation and refuse all the others?" Jerkins interjected officiously.

"You may, Jerkins; but whether I shall actually do so is entirely at my own discretion," she said with suppressed hauteur.

Jerkins was not the least intimidated. "Lady Jersey's parties are commonly known as the creme de la creme of *ton* parties; they are fashionable and lavish events you will undoubtedly be delighted to attend. Not so Lady Mortimer's Ridotto, an annual event open to the general public and notorious for providing entertainment for those demi-mondes who are not normally invited to the *haut ton's* exclusive events. As the daughter of an earl, you have no doubt received this invitation to give the event a more respectable air. I strongly advise you not to fall for it. And Lady Rathke's invitation to dinner is negligible, for you hardly know the lady."

"Thank you, Jerkins, for your unsolicited opinion, which I shall no doubt consider with great care."

But Avery's sarcasm was lost on him as he continued blithely. "Indeed, my lady. One does well to exercise a modicum of caution at even the most fashionable *ton* events. Even Lady Jersey's parties have a tendency to lapse into the raucous once the hour has passed midnight."

"Indeed?"

"Yes, it is undoubtedly the punch that is responsible for the general sense of hilarity and drunkenness that reaches its zenith after midnight. You would do well to stay away from it. Bear in mind also that you will have a rather long journey back to London afterwards, so I would advise you to attend the rout no longer than an hour before returning home."

"Jerkins. Have you quite finished telling me what to do?"

"Yes, my lady. Of course, one must bear in mind—"

"Jerkins," she sighed. "You are incorrigible."

"Yes, my lady."

"Do you think..." She traced the pattern of the finely embroidered tablecloth with a finger, "do you think, er, that Blackshurst will be attending the rout?"

"Unlikely, my lady," he replied promptly.

"Oh? Why?"

"Because I have it on good authority that his lordship is otherwise engaged."

"Ah." Avery blinked, confused. "I wonder what he does when he is not, as you say, attending one of the most fashionable and lavish events in the *ton*."

"I wouldn't know for sure, my lady, but rumour has it that he resides in The Clarendon and spends his time in certain disreputable gambling dens."

Avery looked at him closely to see if he was joking, but his face was as straight as ever.

"Well. That certainly sounds unsavoury."

"Aye, as is his character. Which is why I would advise you to stay away from him."

"Jerkins!" Avery didn't know whether to laugh or get angry.

He bowed. "At your service, my lady."

She would not, of course, take any of his advice. She would attend Lady Jersey's rout, for how could she not? The Ridotto al Fresco as well, which sounded delightful, despite Jerkins's attempt to talk her out of it. As for dinner with Lady Rathke, she would have to see.

She pulled out her Never List and crossed off several items.

Avery hummed to herself as she climbed the stairs to her dressing room.

Chapter Nineteen

LADY JERSEY'S ROUT PARTY WAS HELD AT OSTERLEY Park, her country estate to the west of London. The red-brick mansion with turrets and a white portico with Corinthian columns was grand and imposing.

Accompanied by Belinda, Avery walked through the torch-lit courtyard to the magnificent entrance hall, painted in French grey and white, with niches housing Greek statues and elaborate stucco ceilings. Massive urns stood in each corner of the room.

She looked around with delight.

"Welcome to my home." Lord and Lady Jersey stood at the entrance, greeting the guests. "I'm delighted to have you here, Lady Avery." Lady Jersey nodded regally at Belinda. "Mrs Wimplethorpe. There is only one rule here: you must enjoy yourselves!"

"What a wonderful home you have, Lady Jersey." Avery placed her hand in her outstretched one.

"Sally. Please. We are not to remain on formality tonight! I am so glad you are here."

Soft music floated from the gallery beyond, where some people were dancing. But as this was primarily a rout, most people were standing around in the crowded rooms or playing at the various faro tables that had been set up.

"Faro!" Belinda clapped her hands. "There's no game I like more."

She immediately joined several players gathered around a green baize-covered table. A man shuffled the cards and spread thirteen of them face up on the table. Each player placed their bet on a card with chips.

"Will you join us, Avery?" Belinda looked at her as her fingers closed on a pile of chips.

Avery shook her head. "I'll just watch."

People were playing with real money here. To her shock, she saw that instead of chips, some of the ladies were placing jewellery on the cards—pearl earrings and gold rings, even an emerald brooch. It must be very valuable. Others placed slips of paper.

"Lord Westerly is offering his horse as a stake," Belinda murmured in her ear. She placed a stack of chips on a card—and promptly lost.

Lord Westerly took the note and placed it on another card.

"Too bad for me," Belinda said cheerfully, "better luck next time."

"You're a good loser," Avery remarked.

"You have to win more in the next round. It is all part of the enjoyment."

Belinda played and played; sometimes she lost, then

she won it all back. As Avery watched her, realisation dawned: Belinda was a passionate gamestress. Was this why she was absent most nights? This would explain why she was so tired during the day and slept most of the time. Belinda had claimed her tiredness came from insomnia; Avery would swear on their mad king's beard that it came from gambling through the night. That troubled her.

The staggering amounts people were betting gave Avery a queasy feeling in her stomach. She was used to playing a children's version of faro with her nephew in the nursery, where the highest amount they ever wagered was a few pennies.

She soon lost interest, however, and her eyes swept the room.

He wasn't there.

A pang of disappointment settled in her stomach.

"I shall go to the refreshments room as it is getting quite hot here," she told Belinda, who looked up briefly to tell her, "I'll join you shortly," before turning back to the game.

An assortment of delicious sandwiches, cold meats, pastries, jellies, and colourful ices moulded into a variety of shapes greeted her. She helped herself to a glass of orgeat, which tasted infinitely better than what had been on offer at Almack's, and a small sandwich filled with pheasant fillet.

She exchanged a few words with Lady Rathke, who reminded her of the dinner invitation, and also with Lord Grantham, who seemed quite pleased to see her.

As time passed, however, the rooms became more

crowded, until it was impossible to turn around without ramming one's elbow into someone. Avery worked her way back to the faro table, only to find that Belinda was no longer there.

Why was she not surprised?

Glancing at the clock, she saw that the hour was approaching midnight, and with a suppressed grin, she remembered Jerkins's suggestion that she retire early.

He may have been right, for the tone of the party was becoming decidedly more boisterous. More than one person appeared to be drunk, yet the champagne continued to flow freely.

Avery slipped through the front door into the court-yard and took a deep breath of the clean, fresh country air.

She leaned against one of the columns under the portico and thought back over the past few weeks. Never in her wildest imagination had she thought she'd be invited to parties like this. She'd danced at one ball, with many more to come. She'd been invited to teas and dinners, picnics, and masquerades. She'd been to the theatre and the opera, seen the Elgin Marbles and the waxworks.

She should be content.

Then why this restlessness?

She rubbed her bare arms as a chill blew through the portico.

"Ah, there you are." Lord Grantham stepped towards her. "I've been looking for you, Lady Avery. May I invite you to an exclusive game?" His teeth gleamed white in the moonlight as he smiled.

"I'm afraid I'm not much of a gambler," she said. It was getting late, and she wanted to go home, provided she could find Belinda. "Besides, this is becoming somewhat too riotous for my taste."

"I quite understand. It would be in a separate room entirely, away from the general crowd and noisy commotion. It is quiet there. Come, join us, if only to sit with us and watch us play." He offered her his arm with a gallant bow.

After a moment's hesitation, she accepted.

He led her into a room at the end of the corridor. It was a lovely yellow-accented room. It must be the music room, for there was a harp in the corner and a piano pushed aside to make room for several card tables.

People sat at a card table, surrounded by groups of people watching. The room was full, but not as full as the packed rooms outside. It was quiet except for the clatter of dice on the tables.

It took her a glance to realise they were indeed playing deep.

A new hand was forming on a table by the window.

"Come, let us join, Lady Avery. It's a round of hazard." Lord Grantham offered her a seat.

"Innocent enough." She had played this game with the boys and was not bad at it, but she hesitated.

"Join us," said a gentleman with short grey hair. He rattled the dice in the cup.

"Your Grace, may I present Lady Avery Heywood? Lady Avery, this is His Grace, the Duke of Sommerville." Grantham said.

"Sit down," Sommerville said. "Let's play."

She had never played with real money.

Another thing to cross off her list. "Very well."

The first two rounds went well, and she won a staggering amount that left her speechless.

From then on, her luck began to slide. The stakes were raised higher and higher, to the point where she lost it all on a single hand. She gasped as Grantham, without so much as batting an eyelid, bet what must have been his entire fortune. Sommerville did the same.

She felt quite ill.

"I must withdraw," said Avery.

"But Lady Avery," Grantham said with a smile. "So early? We haven't even started the real game."

"The r-real game?"

"Why, yes. The first few rounds were just to warm up. Now we shall play what we are really here for."

"I'm afraid I am not nearly as skilled a player. Besides, I have nothing to offer."

Grantham leaned back in his chair and looked at her through half-closed lids. There was a smile on his lips that she did not like at all.

"But you do, Lady Avery."

Her hand went to the pearl necklace that adorned her neck. Belinda had lent it to her. She could not gamble it away; it would be unforgivable.

"I couldn't possibly."

Grantham's eyes fell on her necklace, but he shook his head. "Paltry. Why not offer something of far greater value?"

"Such as?"

"Yourself."

Avery stared at him. He must be drunk. He had indeed been holding a champagne glass between his fingers all evening, and there was a slight slur in his speech, but he bore the alcohol well, so she hadn't noticed he was drunk until now.

She licked her lips, which he watched with interest. "I don't understand."

"Now here's an excellent suggestion," Sommerville said, leaning forward. There was a leering grin on his lean face. "A night with Lady Avery. That will add some spice to the game. For what is an entire estate—or your entire fortune—worth in comparison?"

Avery's stomach dropped to the floor. She shook her head wildly. "No."

It was indecent. It was shockingly inappropriate. It just wasn't done.

"Come, come, Lady Avery." Grantham leaned back in his chair. "Why not take fate by the hand and see where it takes you? Who knows, you could walk out of this room richer than you ever imagined, with an estate to boot. You'd never have to worry about a thing in your life again. Take a chance! Surely you have never done anything like this before."

Avery sat up as if stung by a bee.

Surely, she had *never* done anything like this before...

No, she had not.

She must be touched in the head to even consider this for longer than a second.

Suppose she won.

What would she do with all that money?

The freedom she'd have. She would never have to depend on anyone again. She'd travel the world and live wherever she wanted, do whatever she wanted.

She wouldn't be dependent on living with her relatives anymore.

She'd be a spinster, yes, but at least she'd be a rich spinster. And no one could ever tell her what to do. Ever.

"Very well." Her breath caught.

A broad grin spread across Grantham's face. "Excellent." He handed her a piece of paper and a pencil. She wrote down her wager, which was herself.

Grantham was the caster. He chose the main, the number seven. "My lucky number." He grinned, then rattled the ivory dice in the wooden cup. He rolled the dice. It was an eight. That number would be his "chance." If, in the second round, he hit the chance, he would nick, or win the game. If he rolled the main, a seven, he'd lose, and she'd get her stake back, in addition to being rich for life.

The dice rattled in the cup. He cast them.

Avery watched the little white cubes skitter across the table. Her heart pounded in her ears.

She stared at the dots on the dice and saw black dots dancing across her vision.

He'd rolled an eight.

She felt sick.

"Lucky devil," Sommerville growled. "Well, I'll get over it. At least I have two estates left."

Avery looked at the dice in horror. What had she done?

Grantham looked at her like a cat who'd licked a bowl of cream. "Lady Avery. You're mine."

"Not quite," a smooth voice broke through. "I'm doubling the stakes. In return for your winnings."

Avery looked up, straight into Blackshurst's steely eyes.

Chapter Twenty

"BLACKSHURST! THE DEVIL!" GRANTHAM HISSED.

Avery was so relieved she felt dizzy. Thank the heavens he'd decided to come after all! Then she looked at his face and quickly averted her eyes.

He looked like thunder.

"Well?" Blackshurst addressed Grantham coolly.

"Double the stakes?" Grantham narrowed his eyes.

"Make it triple. And I cast." The coldness with which he'd said the words made Avery shiver.

Grantham's fingers played idly with the dice as he considered the offer. Then he pushed the dice across the table towards him.

Silence fell over the room.

She rose from her chair, and Blackshurst took her place.

People gathered around their table.

"Declare your main," Grantham said.

Blackshurst picked up the dice and they clicked together. "Six." He never took his eyes off Grantham.

Grantham nodded and crossed his arms.

Blackshurst rattled the dice in the cup, but instead of throwing them across the table, he trapped them under the cup and pushed them back at Grantham without breaking eye contact.

Avery clenched her sweaty fingers into a fist.

Grantham unfolded his arms and lifted the cup.

A murmur went through the room.

He had rolled the main: a six.

Blackshurst had won with a single throw.

"It's a fair win," Sommerville declared. "He rolled your dice and nicked. Horrendous bad luck for you, Grantham."

Grantham stared at the dice with a pale face.

Blackshurst collected the papers on the table and pushed one towards Sommerville, the other towards Grantham. "Keep them. I only want the woman."

"Dash it, that's more than generous of you," Sommerville spluttered.

"You won it in an honest game," Grantham replied stiffly, not picking up his stake. "It's yours."

"I have no need of it." He turned to Avery and said, "Come."

"Care for another round?" Sommerville asked Grantham. Before he could answer, Blackshurst took Avery by the elbow and led her out of the room.

"Thank you," she stammered. Her knees had turned to butter.

"What for?" he replied coolly.

"It could have ended badly."

"It did end badly. For you. As for me, I have every

intention of claiming my victory." He gave her a wolfish grin.

Avery stared at him, horrified. Surely, he was joking. This was Jerkins, after all. But for a moment he'd quite rattled her, no doubt because he was angry with her, as he probably had every right to be.

Unthinkable how this could have ended if he hadn't shown up.

What had she been thinking?

"Grantham caught me off guard and persuaded me to join him in the gambling room. I had no idea," she swallowed, "no idea what kind of games they play here. It is terrible! And fascinating. And addictive. I never want to do it again."

"Grantham is a hardened gamester, and you are more naive than a duckling. You made it all too easy for him to fleece you. Let that be a lesson to you."

She dropped her head and sadly admitted he was right. It had indeed been a lesson.

He manoeuvred her through the crowd into the hall where Belinda was waiting at the door.

"There you are, Cousin! I was quite worried about you and wondered if I should go alone and ask Lady Jersey to lend you a carriage. Oh!" she exclaimed as she saw Blackshurst holding her arm.

"Where have you been all this time? Aren't you supposed to be chaperoning Lady Avery?" he snapped.

Belinda sputtered.

"Take her home and don't let her out of your sight until she's safely in her bedroom."

Avery turned to protest, but he bowed, turned and left before she could open her mouth.

"Well." Belinda said after she'd closed her mouth. "What was riding him, I wonder?"

Thoroughly chastened by her experience and in a state of turmoil, she sat quietly in the carriage on the way back to London as it rattled along the highway.

She looked out the window, and as the moon broke through the clouds, she imagined she saw a lone horseman on the top of the hill, watching them.

Was it a highwayman?

Suddenly wide awake, she sat up straight and stared out, only for the clouds to dim the moonlight.

When the moon came out again, he was gone.

Maybe she'd just imagined it, but part of her knew that if it was a highwayman, he wasn't there to rob her, but to protect her.

Arriving at Wimpole Street, she was not surprised to see Jerkins at the door, back in his wig and livery.

She had no idea how he'd done it. He must have been riding like a madman.

Avery held up her hand dismissively. "Don't say a word, Jerkins. Not. One. Word."

She swept past him, chin held high, resisting with every fibre of her being the urge to fall into his arms and cry.

He merely raised an eyebrow. "Very well, my lady."

Chapter Twenty-One

For the next few days, Avery refrained from leaving the house, telling Jerkins that she was not at home to anyone. She secluded herself in the study and, when she did not write, stared a hole into the wallpaper. She'd fairly memorised the pattern. There were bees and blue-birds and butterflies on it, and the woodpecker's steep, proud forehead reminded her of Jerkins.

She scowled and looked away.

He was probably in the parlour now, doing whatever it was that butlers did. Not a good time to step outside just yet, lest they run into each other.

She had to wait at least one more hour to be on the safe side.

She felt skittish around him, and she didn't care for the pulsating sensation that unfurled in her chest and the throbbing in her ears every time he was near. It confused her, made her stutter, and then, good heavens, he'd raise his eyebrow and her bones would melt to a sticky puddle, like Gunter's pistachio ice that had been left out too long in the sun. Since that could not be, she avoided him whenever she could and was curt with him when she could not, lest it occur to him to broach the topic of that awful night.

But he never did.

Jerkins went docilely about his butler business as though he'd never touched dice in his entire life, appearing entirely incapable of gambling with such determined, ice-cold calculation.

How was it possible that his placid, steadfast demeanour was but a mask hiding the dangerous, reckless personality of a rakehell and gambler?

Or maybe she had it all wrong and it was the other way around? Maybe Jerkins was who he really was and Blackshurst was the role he played.

How he baffled her!

The best course of action, Avery decided, was not to think about it. She therefore dedicated her time to writing. Her story was coming along nicely, and she was pleased with her progress.

One morning, Jerkins finally caught her in the hallway, appearing out of nowhere as he always did, heading towards her. She'd taken a second too long to decide whether, in a rush of panic, she ought to squeeze between the wall and the longcase pendulum clock or scramble up the stairs on all fours in an undignified manner.

She looked around wildly and found herself trapped.

"Your ladyship." A muscle jumped in his cheek as if repressing a smile. That man knew exactly what she'd been about to do, and why.

"Jerkins." She nodded regally.

"I've read your ladyship's story, and I must say I enjoyed it very much." He handed the manuscript to her. "I am convinced it will be very popular with readers."

"Oh." Avery felt the tight coil in her unwind, and she nearly collapsed with relief. "Did you truly like it?"

"Indeed, very much so."

She clutched the manuscript for support. "You find it entertaining, yes?"

"Certainly. Except," he hesitated for a moment before continuing, "if I may be so bold as to point out one tiny detail that may need correcting. It is purely cosmetic."

She raised an eyebrow. "Oh? What would that be?"

Jerkins folded his hands. "It has to do with the mechanics of holding up a carriage."

"I'm interested. Please continue."

"The story focuses on a single highwayman holding up a mail coach to kidnap the lady inside. You describe him moving his horse into the path of the coach with a pistol drawn."

"Yes. That's how it's done, isn't it?" She gave him a sharp upward glance as she waited for his answer.

"Not exactly. You ought to think of it like this: the highwayman, on his horse, steps into the path of a four-horse coach thundering down the road. It is reasonable to assume that the coachman will stop, otherwise there will be an accident of catastrophic proportions. Very well, so now he has successfully brought the coach to a halt. The highwayman points his gun at the coachman. And?"

Avery blinked. "What do you mean, and? He proceeds to rob the passengers, of course."

"Precisely how can he rob the passengers in the coach?"

She cocked her head to one side. "As I wrote in my story. He just robs them."

"Yes, but how, exactly? Remember, he must point the pistol at the coachman. Suppose he moves his horse from the front to the side of the coach to point it at the passengers to induce them to hand over their valuables. Supposing you were the coachman, what would you do now?"

She stared at him wide-eyed. "Now that the way is clear, I would urge the horses to a gallop and escape."

"Exactly. You would run. Anyone in their right mind would. And your highwayman wouldn't have much chance of robbing the coach, would he? For you've also forgotten the guard sitting in the dickey seat at the back, guarding the mailbox. He'd probably be armed to the teeth with pistols and a blunderbuss. Your highwayman really has no chance. He'd be a dead man before he could say 'stand and deliver' and that would be the end of your story."

"How utterly vexatious." Avery bit her lower lip and thought for a moment. After a while she threw up her hands. "I've never robbed a mail coach before, so how would I know how to do it right?" She glared at Jerkins as if it was his fault.

He smiled. "Let us sum it up. You need a pistol pointed at the coachman lest he bolts. Then you need another one aimed at the guard in the rear, who is highly dangerous and armed. And then you need one for the passengers to make them hand over their valuables. That makes three pistols. While it is likely that your intrepid highwayman carries that many pistols on his person—and if he is clever, he will, especially if they are flintlocks with only one shot each—they would take far too long to reload. It is unlikely that he will grow a third arm to hold a pistol at three different people in different places. Ergo, the only solution is for him to work—"

"—with others," she breathed.

"Aye. Highwaymen usually work with gangs. Even Dick Turpin worked with the notorious Essex gang."

"Jax Tyrrell?"

Jerkins shrugged. "How else would he have been so successful at highway robbery? Didn't we just establish that it's impossible for one person to accomplish that feat alone?"

"But the legends never mention that! They only ever celebrate the single highwayman."

"I assume we may conclude that the legends are wrong?"

Avery looked at him darkly. "But I want a lone highwayman holding up a coach! It's more romantic that way!"

"Yes, well, of course you may do whatever you want to do, since you are the author, and you may write whatever pleases you. But if we were to ask if it was realistic, then I suppose there would be some arguments as to why your vision of a mail coach being robbed might not exactly work."

She groaned. "Once again, Jerkins, you have ruined a perfectly good story."

"I don't see why. Just add a few more highwaymen and have them work in a gang."

Avery glared at him. "It's not as easy as you say. It means creating and developing new characters. How and where would they even meet to coordinate their heinous plans?"

"At Halfway House, in all likelihood."

"Halfway House. What is that? It sounds wonderfully sinister."

"A very disreputable coaching inn just after Knightsbridge on the road to Bath. Highwaymen used to gather there to spy on passing coaches and decide which ones to rob later."

"Fascinating. One moment." She held up a finger, went to the study, pulled out a piece of paper and her pen and returned. "I need to take notes. Gang work. Halfway house. These are all extremely interesting details that I would like to include in my story."

"I dare say it's only natural that your ladyship should be unfamiliar with the details of robbing a coach. But it is common knowledge that one is well advised not to stop at Halfway House. The coaches still tend to gallop past it as if they have the devil on their heels, which they very well might. And I have merely told you all this because after your ill-fated expedition to the Angel Inn, I trust you will have enough common sense not to venture out on your own to visit it yourself. It is a bad place. Worse than the Angel Inn." He frowned.

"As I said, fascinating." She gave him a brooding look. "You are a man of mysterious depths and talents. If you ever feel like you need to change your occupation, you would do very well as an actor, since you seem very adept at slipping in and out of various roles."

"Oh no, my lady. I am quite content in my current occupation. Besides, I suffer from terrible stage fright."

She uttered a small laugh. "I still feel I owe you a debt of gratitude."

There, she'd finally acknowledged it, albeit somewhat grudgingly. It was true, he'd saved her from a sticky spot, and she owed him her gratitude. She'd just struggled to find the right words up until now.

But he brushed her aside. "Speaking of the devil, the earl has sent another bouquet of roses." He did not pull a muscle in his face.

She laughed. "Jerkins, you're incorrigible. Bring them in."

This time there was a note with the roses, scrawled in black ink. "I will claim my wager tomorrow night at Almack's. B."

Avery drew in her breath sharply as ice-cold heat coursed through her veins. Goodness! If that didn't set her heart off pounding again. What did Jerkins mean by that? Surely there was no need for him to prolong the game this way.

She peered at the note. If this was Jerkins/Black-shurst's handwriting, it didn't match the notebook she'd found. Unless Jerkins had asked someone else to write it for him.

Almack's.

Avery bit her lower lip. She had no intention of going to Almack's tomorrow night. Instead, she'd be going to the Ridotto al Fresco at Vauxhall, but she'd never tell the disapproving Jerkins. Belinda was informed and thought it a splendid plan.

She smiled. Blackshurst would have to wait to claim his wager. And while it had been a relief to have him save her from a predicament at Lady Jersey's rout, and she was indeed grateful for his intervention, she would prefer to go to a ball without her horribly efficient, omnipresent butler watching her.

Chapter Twenty-Two

WHEN BELINDA AND AVERY STEPPED OFF THE BOAT at Vauxhall Gardens, they could hear the music and laughter from afar. Hundreds of little lanterns lit up the garden, transforming it into a magical place. To the left and right were pillared semi-circular piazzas with supper boxes, and in the middle of the grove stood an octagonal building where the orchestra played. The atmosphere was one of exuberance and gaiety.

Avery enjoyed being incognito behind her mask. It gave her a sense of freedom that others did not know who she was. Everyone was in costume: shepherdesses, goddesses, Elizabethan courtiers, and Oriental pashas. It was exciting and overwhelming, colourful, and noisy.

It was also just as Jerkins had predicted: slightly scandalous. Since everyone was disguised, class distinctions were blurred. The aristocracy freely mingled with the lower classes, and social etiquette was thrown into the wind. Formal introductions were not required to dance with each other. Although, a little voice told her, it was not a prudent thing to do, and one had best not dance with complete strangers. Then she brushed those thoughts away, for she was here to dance, dance, dance, all night long.

Belinda, as expected, threw herself into the fray, and although Avery tried to cling to her sleeve so as not to lose her, they were separated within ten minutes of entering the square.

To her delight, a tall Roman emperor immediately asked her to dance, which she readily accepted.

The Scottish reel left her breathless. Afterwards, his Imperial Majesty was kind enough to bring her some lemonade, which she drank gratefully.

"You dance well." He was a tall, slender man, and no doubt a gentleman, for he treated her with courtesy.

"Thank you, as do you," Avery replied.

"Would you like to dance again?" he offered as the music started again.

To dance twice in a row with the same gentleman was certainly frowned upon at other balls.

"I would love to—" Avery began but was interrupted by a deep, hollow-sounding male voice behind her.

"I believe this dance is mine."

Avery's heart lurched and dropped to the floor.

Blackshurst!

He was dressed in a black domino and wore a Venetian mask that covered the entire upper half of his face. It had a beak, similar to the mask medieval plague doctors had worn, but not quite as long. He held out his hand.

Silently, she let herself be led to her place in the next set.

She danced a country dance with him, but halfway through he pulled her out of the set. With her hand in his, he led her away from the square and through the wooded grove into the shady lanes.

"Where are we going?" she asked breathlessly. His grip was too tight, and she had to run to keep up with his steps.

He did not answer.

The music had faded, and it was cool between the trees. There was only the sound of gravel crunching under their feet.

Suddenly, he stopped and whirled around.

She smelled his enticing cologne: bergamot, musk, and lemon. She would have known the scent anywhere.

Without warning, he grabbed her by the shoulders and pressed his mouth on hers.

Avery's first thought was one of jubilation: Finally, she was being kissed!

Her second thought was one of wonder: So, this is what it felt like.

Her third thought was: Wet. Very wet.

She fidgeted.

She couldn't breathe.

Her nose was pressed against the side of the beak of his Venetian mask, which was poking into her cheek. His mouth groped, his tongue probed, and her teeth clashed against his. He also had bad breath.

Avery came to the definite conclusion that kissing was an altogether unpleasant practice. What on earth did people see in it? There were too many sharp elbows, teeth, and chins involved, and she began to get a cramp in her neck from holding her head sideways.

His fingers dug into her shoulders, and she began to squirm. When he clamped his arms around her to invade her mouth further, she decided she'd had enough.

She pushed against his chest, pulled her head away from his groping mouth, then threw it up and cracked it right into his chin.

He staggered back, stumbling over a root. "What did you do that for?" he growled.

"I have had enough and would like to be taken back to the piazza immediately." Avery glared at him.

She felt a flare of anger at Jerkins. Not only was he a terrible kisser, but he'd manhandled her. She would have bruises on her shoulders.

When he didn't react immediately, she turned her back to him and stomped back to the main alley, muttering under her breath.

Several giggling couples appeared from behind the trees, and Avery stepped out of their way. These couples evidently had kissed as well but enjoyed the activity. That left her even more grumpy.

"Really, Blackshurst. I don't know what you were thinking..." she turned to glare at him, only to find that the alley behind her was empty.

It wasn't supposed to be like this.

Her first kiss should have been a romantic, unforgettable experience, the memory of which would warm the cold winter nights she spent cooped up in the country with Great-Aunt Euphemia. Instead, she was left with a strong feeling of disgust and unease.

Just what, if you please, had that been all about?

How could she ever look Jerkins in the eye again? Shame and humiliation washed over her. She felt she could no longer trust him, and that thought made her heart sink like lead to the bottom of her stomach.

She angrily wiped the tears from her cheeks.

Where was a handkerchief when one needed it?

And where was Cousin Belinda?

They'd agreed to meet at the entrance to the pleasure garden if they were inevitably separated. Avery worked her way through the crowd to the gate and waited.

It was dark, and the crowd had changed. Lewdly dressed women hung onto the arms of drunken gentlemen; couples were ensconced in the dark nooks, kissing. More than one man threw a leering glance in her direction.

For the first time, she was aware that her lack of a male companion put her in a vulnerable position. But of what use were male companions if they attempted to take advantage?

Belinda reappeared after half an hour, without a mask and out of breath.

"I've had enough, Cousin," she declared. "Someone stepped on my dress and tore off half the trim. And I lost my mask in the fray. Let us go home."

Avery agreed. They took the boat back and climbed into the carriage that would take them home.

IT WAS FRED, the footman, who opened the door.

"Someone is awaiting you in the drawing room, my lady," he said with a grin and a twinkle in his eye.

Avery groaned. "So late? It's almost midnight."

She threw open the door and scowled at the gentleman lounging on the sofa. He was dressed in black evening clothes and seemed to be studying his fingernails as she burst into the room.

"I have no idea how you did it, but I have quite enough for tonight. Your behaviour has been abominable. Inexcusable! And then, instead of escorting us home safely, you bolted and decided to return alone, only to find yourself here before me. The nerve!"

Blackshurst rose from the sofa and listened to her tirade with folded arms. A frown creased his forehead.

"Please repeat that, Lady Avery. I did what?"

She waved her hands around. "You know. Showing up like this, interrupting a perfectly nice conversation with the Roman Emperor, asking me, no, demanding me to dance with you."

"Ah."

"And then, in the middle of the dance, dragging me off in that indecorous manner into the dark alleys where couples go to engage in all sorts of lewd behaviour."

"Very unseemly indeed. And what did I do then?"

This made Avery even more angry. "Don't talk as if you didn't know exactly what you did next! Really. You're a terrible kisser."

She crossed her arms and scowled.

There was a pause during which Blackshurst looked at her with a disquieting glint in his eyes. "Is that so?" he asked, so softly that the fine hairs on her arm stood on end.

"Y-yes." She swallowed.

"And tell me"—he took a step towards her, causing her to take an involuntary step back and her leg knocked against the small side table—"tell me, what did I do then?" His voice was silky.

"Y-you pulled me into your arms." There was nowhere to go. If she took another step back, the Ming vase on the table would topple. She was cornered.

He took her hand and pulled her to the sofa, where he sat down. "Like this?" He tugged her onto his lap.

"N-not exactly."

Why did she allow him to even touch her? She had no intention of repeating the experience. But it was as if his voice put her in a trance, and her limbs no longer obeyed her brain. He held her gently, but in a firm, warm embrace, and she melted against his hard, warm body. The man radiated heat like a furnace.

"And then?" he asked softly.

"And th-then you k-k-kissed me." She bent her head away. If he kissed her again, she would not only jam her head into his chin, but stick her elbow into his stomach.

He lifted a finger and turned her chin towards him. "May I kiss you, Avery?"

She looked into his eyes, drowning in a sea of fiery silver desire. And something else, deep down. It was a wistful tenderness, like the look he'd given her the day she thought she was leaving. As if he thought she was infinitely precious, but beyond his reach. It made her catch her breath in wonder.

She knew without a doubt that if she said no, he would drop his hands and let her go.

She also knew that if she said no, she would forever-more regret it.

So, she gave a curt nod, pressed her eyes shut and waited, her pulse skittering alarmingly.

He pressed a gentle kiss on her forehead. "Did I kiss you here?"

She opened her eyes in wonder. "No."

He bent his head and planted a kiss on the pulsing hollow of her throat. "Did I kiss you there?" His voice was thick.

"No," Avery breathed. Every fibre in her body tingled.

He nibbled at her left earlobe. "Here, maybe?"

She let out a strangled moan.

Then his lips brushed against hers, lighter than the whisper of a butterfly's wing. Once, twice, so tender it was unbearable.

"Did I kiss you like that?" he asked, out of breath.

Avery's hand went to her lips. "No," she whispered.

He reclaimed her lips in a slow, drugging, exploratory kiss.

Avery felt her bones turn to water, then fire.

She took a deep breath of his cologne and froze.

Blackshurst lifted his head to look at her inquisitively.

"You never went to the Ridotto in Vauxhall Gardens, did you?" Avery asked.

He played with a curl that hung down her neck. "No, I didn't. But whoever did must have done so deliberately to fool you into thinking he was me. My bottle of cologne was stolen during the break-in. It is a special blend that has been mixed for me. We can safely conclude that whoever broke into the house was the man at Vauxhall. Describe him. From the beginning."

She told him how she'd arrived with Belinda, how she'd been asked to dance, and how the man she thought was him had interrupted and demanded to dance with her. She described him as best she could, but it had been dark, and his voice had sounded strange.

"He was wearing a mask," she explained. "And I suppose I was horribly gullible. But part of me expected you to be there; I expected you to appear and ask me to dance. So, when a gentleman of your stature and wearing your cologne appeared, I did not think twice. Foolish of me, I know. I vow I shall not repeat this mistake."

"I should have known you would sneak off to the ridotto against my express advice," Blackshurst said. "You enjoy doing the opposite of what I tell you." He softened his words by resting his chin on her head.

Avery nestled against him with a sigh. "Have you been waiting here all evening?"

"I expected to see you at Almack's, as agreed, but by the time I realised you weren't there it was too late. It was not easy to get away from there. When I returned and you were still not there, I concluded you must have gone to Vauxhall. I was on the point of following you when you returned. After all, you still owe me my wager," he growled.

She shivered with delight. "Haven't you already claimed it with those kisses?"

"Not nearly enough."

"I'm sorry. You were right. It was not what I expected.

I should have gone to Almack's and danced with you. There is one thing I don't understand: why? None of this makes any sense. Who is he and what does he want?"

He clenched his hands and stayed silent for so long, Avery wondered if he'd heard her. "I have enemies, Avery. And you were caught in the crossfire. Did he hurt you?"

She hesitated, thinking of her bruised shoulder. "Just my pride," she finally admitted.

"He's a dead man," he said savagely.

She shivered. He sounded so different. Neither Jerkins nor Blackshurst, but another man altogether.

"Who are you?" she whispered. "And why are we playing this game?"

"My love." He leaned his forehead against hers. "There will be answers. I promise. If only you could learn to trust me a little more."

She had so many questions. Why? And what was this all about? And who was he, really? Instead, she asked the most important question of all:

"Regarding that wager. Could you kiss me again? If you please."

Chapter Twenty-Three

AFTER THE FIASCO AT VAUXHALL GARDENS, AVERY found herself unexpectedly weary of the glittering events of the *ton*. The allure of those society events, once a source of fascination, now seemed to wane. Blackshurst was conspicuously absent, and Jerkins was not at home much, either. His whereabouts remained shrouded in mystery.

Where did he keep going and what was he up to?

The memory of that evening evoked a quickening of her pulse as she recalled the touch of his lips upon hers. She found herself, more than once, staring dreamily into the distance, reliving every moment.

Trust me, he'd said.

But how could one trust someone when one did not know who they were?

One morning, the footman brought her a note.

"An errand boy just delivered this." He held it out to her. "He wouldn't say who it was from."

"Thank you, Fred." When the footman had gone, she

opened the black blob of wax that sealed it. It was written in spidery handwriting:

Lady Avry
    If you want to know the truth about your butler cum to Halfway House tomorrow evening Alone

THE 'ALONE' was underlined twice. It was unsigned.

"Well!" Her head whirled. What did this mean? Who could it be?

One thing was clear: whoever wrote this had no concept of spelling or punctuation.

And why did the sender assume she'd have no qualms about going to the Halfway House on her own? Because of course she would do no such thing. It was foolish. She'd end up getting herself kidnapped, or worse.

Didn't Jerkins say the other day that Halfway House was the most disreputable inn in the kingdom? Or something to that effect. He'd also told her not to go there on her own.

She put the note down on the table and smoothed the paper.

If you want to know the truth about your butler...

It was very tempting, for she did want to know the truth.

But no. It was impossible.

No respectable lady would ever set foot in that inn.

Then again, she'd set foot in another equally disreputable inn, and she'd been fine.

Avery tugged at her lower lip. But Emma had been with her then, and apart from discovering that the innkeeper there was a rude boor, she'd discovered nothing. The note confirmed her suspicion that there was a connection between her butler and the world of highwaymen.

She had no idea how or in what capacity.

Her eyes returned to the spidery handwriting on the note. If she went to Halfway Inn, she could finally get some answers.

It was a dangerous venture. She was mad as a March hare to even consider it. But it would be an adventure!

She'd *never* had a proper adventure.

Her heartbeat quickened.

She could make sure she was safe. The coachman would be armed. She herself could take a pistol in a bag.

She would get some answers, and she would remain safe.

In the evening of the next day, Avery told Fred to call her a hackney.

Armed with the pistol from her brother's cabinet in a small tapestry bag, she climbed into the coach.

She wore a dark cloak over her head, hiding her light hair.

Halfway House Inn was not far from Hyde Park Turnpike, a nondescript, run-down inn with a rickety stable attached to the side. From the smell of it, it housed pigs as well as horses.

She dismounted and told the coachman to wait for her here, and if she did not return in half an hour, to go in and fetch her.

Lifting her skirts and cloak to avoid the mud and horse droppings, she stepped up to the inn and pushed the door open.

It was dark inside, more gloomy, musty, and smoky than the Angel Inn. Little wooden tables were arranged in a ramshackle manner in the small, tight taproom.

To her surprise, a woman stood behind the bar. She was tall and stocky, with arms as thick as tree trunks. Her hair was tied back with a scarf and a pipe dangled from the corner of her mouth.

Once Avery had recovered from her surprise, she stepped up to the counter.

The woman looked her up and down. "Ah. Your ladyship's arrived. 'E's waiting for ye in that corner." She poked her chin into a dark corner of the room.

"Who?" she asked.

The woman just laughed. "Y'll see."

As Avery walked around the room and through the tables, she felt as if every single pair of eyes were on her.

She licked her lips and gripped her tapestry bag so tightly between her fingers that her knuckles turned white.

There was a table in a dark corner of the room, but it was empty.

She turned, confused. Where was he? Certainly not the old, spindly man sitting on the table next to her, drinking a pint of beer and grinning at her with no teeth at all.

"He's waiting for you outside," the old man said after wiping his lips with the back of his hand.

"Outside?"

"Aye." The man pointed to a small wooden door that looked like a back exit.

The best course of action at this point would be to return to her own carriage.

As if reading her mind, the old man leaned forward. "If you go, you'll get your answers."

"And what would you know?" Avery countered.

"Me? I know nothing." The old man shrugged and ignored her as he continued to drink his beer.

What on earth should she do? Venture through yonder sinister-looking door? Or simply return home and never know what might have happened?

There it was again: never. Never to know. Never to take the risk. Never to brave one's fears.

She straightened her shoulders and raised her chin. She had sworn that the word 'never' would no longer rule her life, hadn't she?

She wanted answers, and she would get them.

Avery stepped through the door.

She almost tripped over a squealing piglet that ran in front of her feet. She found herself in a very dirty yard, with pigs, chickens, and a cow running around loose, and a carriage waiting at the door.

"Lady Avery?" the coachman said to her. "You're being awaited in the carriage."

She shook her head. "No."

Ignoring her protest, the coachman opened the door. A man sat in the shadowy corner of the coach.

"I'll wait out here and we'll talk like this. Or, even better, why don't you come out and we'll talk outside?" she suggested.

"'Too dangerous," a low voice replied.

Avery recognised the voice at once.

It was the man from Vauxhall Gardens.

She took a step back and bumped into the coachman, who suddenly grabbed her by the arms and lifted her into the carriage as if she were a sack of turnips.

The horses started galloping before the door even slammed shut. Avery staggered into the seat opposite the shadowy figure. Panic shot through her and froze her mind, and she could not think clearly.

"'There is no use resisting," the voice said, bored. "If you scream, you will be rendered insensible. And that would be rather dull for me, for I'd prefer to talk, as I am certain you do."

"Where are you taking me?" Avery's entire body shook with fear, but she gripped the edge of the seat tightly for support.

"Not too far from here. No harm will come to you if you remain calm."

Avery fought the impulse to rip open the door and throw herself out onto the road. That would be foolish, for she would surely break her neck doing so, as the horses were galloping at full speed.

"My coachman is waiting for me, and he has instructions to come after me if I have not returned in half an hour."

"No, he won't," the man replied. "He took off without so much as a peep after being handed a bag of coins."

She gasped. "You bribed him!"

"Naturally. A fair and square deal. Now, Lady Avery.

I suppose you have all sorts of questions, which I shall answer forthwith. How may I be of service?"

She considered drawing her pistol, then decided it was too soon. First, some answers. Her mind whirled. "Before we talk about my questions, I would like to know why you are so eager to convey me the information I seek. I cannot believe you are so selfless as to merely provide me with information. What do you want in return?"

Her heart thundered so loudly that she was sure he could hear it.

The man chuckled. "You are very keen, Lady Avery. I do indeed have a vested interest in this matter. It requires the recounting of a long tale."

"Why in this carriage? And where are you taking me?"

"Never fear, for as I said, no harm shall befall you. May I felicitate you by saying your demeanour hitherto has been lacking entirely in hysterics?" His eyes gleamed in the darkness.

How on earth she had ever mistaken him for Jerkins was beyond her. It was certainly dusky in the coach, but she could tell he was not as tall as Jerkins; he also seemed slimmer, wirier. He spoke with a kind of affected, stilted English that did not seem to come naturally to him.

Yet he was polite, and so far, he had not touched her.

She remembered the awful kiss he'd forced on her in Vauxhall and her hand clenched around her bag again. "Very well. We will talk like civilised people. But if you touch me again, I will kill you."

The man chuckled. "Never fear. That kiss was only

for amusement. I have no interest in you except as a pawn."

"A pawn?"

"Yes. But first, allow me to introduce myself." He lifted his hat. "I am what some would call a highwayman. And the man you call Jerkins, your butler, was my accomplice."

He bowed. "Jax Tyrrell at your service."

Chapter Twenty-Four

"No," Avery breathed. "It can't be. Jax Tyrrell is dead. I visited his grave myself."

"Did you, now? How honoured I am. I am happy to inform you that Jax Tyrrell is alive and breathing and talking to you right now." His white teeth gleamed in the darkness.

"How?"

"Someone else hung in my place."

"How is that even possible?"

"My dear. You'd be surprised to learn about what is possible in this corrupt world of ours. Of course, poor, insignificant John the pickpocket, who had done nothing out of the ordinary all his life except steal a horse and get caught for it, was only too happy to go to the gallows under the name of a legendary highwayman who was celebrated high and low. He was given expensive clothes, a fine meal, and the promise that his wife and children would be looked after. He died a quick and jolly death."

"So that's how you did it," Avery breathed. "I understand you managed to fool the public, but the entire legal system? The lawyers and judges?"

He waved it away. "Anything is possible if you have a deep enough pocket with which to bribe people."

"I can't believe the system is that corrupt."

"As I said, anything is possible. But let us not go into the details. What interests me more"—he leaned forward as he rested his arms on his knees—"is how that bloody butler of yours managed to fool you."

Jerkins. Yes. That was why she was here. "Tell me about Jerkins." She clutched her skirts in her hands.

"Jerkins." He shook his head with a chuckle. "May he rot in hell. He was also a highwayman, did you know?"

Avery's stomach sank to the floor. She wondered why she was so surprised to hear him confirm something she had long suspected herself. "I had my suspicions."

"We worked together, quite efficiently. He held up the coach, and I robbed the passengers. Then I would hold up the next coach and he would rob the ladies of their jewellery. He was quite a ladies' man in his day."

"I can imagine," Avery murmured. "You and he, and possibly two or three other men, formed a gang of highwaymen."

"You've got a very bright head on your shoulders, don't you?"

"What happened next?"

"We shared the spoils."

The notebook. Jerkins had kept a record of everything they'd taken.

"And that's where things didn't go so well, I suppose."

"Excellent brains, my lady. Your wonderful Jerkins

was beginning to develop some scruples. I dare say it was because he'd fallen for a woman, hard, and wanted out. But once a highwayman, always a highwayman."

The whites of his eyes shone in the dark, causing Avery to repress an involuntary shiver.

"We got on well, he and I, and I dare say it would have stayed that way if he hadn't started taking things that didn't belong to him."

"Forgive me, but one would assume that the role of a highwayman is to take things that are not his to take," Avery said dryly.

"Yes. Material things. Money. Jewellery and the like. But not women."

"Are you saying he kidnapped women? I would say that this seems to be your particular accomplishment." She could not see his face exactly, but she had the feeling he was scowling.

"The blackguard took *my* woman, which he had no right to do."

"What happened?" Avery's fingers crawled into the opening of her carpet bag as he told his story.

"Your Jerkins was a womaniser. He just couldn't resist them. A vexatious thing indeed when you're all set to fleece the people in a coach, and here you have your colleague wooing the female passengers. Flirting with them, promising not to take their pearl necklaces if they gave him a kiss." He snorted.

"Just like Claude DuVall." That seventeenth-century gentleman highwayman had gained notoriety for his charm and susceptibility to female charms. Once, when a passenger pulled out her recorder flute to play a tune, no doubt to distract him, DuVall was said to have pulled out his own instrument and played the accompanying tune. He then asked her to dance and demanded payment from her husband for the entertainment. Avery knew the story well, as she'd often told it to her nephews.

"Aye, Claude DuVall was his big idol, the fool. We could have taken twice as much booty if he hadn't insisted on being so gentlemanly with the fairer sex. As if that wasn't enough conflict, he had to make Molly fall in love with him."

Avery's fingers touched the cold metal of the pistol and moved slowly to the hilt. "Tell me about Molly."

"She was a prime article. The most beautiful woman to walk the face of the earth. Black hair like velvet, lips like cherries, and a bosom to die for."

A pang of jealousy stabbed Avery's heart.

"She was an innkeeper's daughter. A happier, livelier thing never lived, and she was mine. She promised to marry me if I would stop the highway robbery. She said I could take over the inn. I told her we could have a leg-shackle as soon as I'd collected enough for us to make a good living for the rest of our lives. I'd become a boring innkeeper, like she wanted, and live happily ever after in the inn with her, with three or four children. Yes, that was her dream. That was our dream."

"And then?"

"And then she met him," he spat, "and he took one look at her and decided he wanted her. And he got her. Stole her from me, and all my dreams with her."

Of course he would have fallen for that exuberant dark-haired beauty who was everything she was not,

Avery concluded, and the slithering snake in the pit of her stomach agreed.

She pressed a finger between her brows. "I don't understand much about these things, but you'd think you couldn't just 'get' a lady if you wanted her; she'd at least have to want you back or have fallen in love with you as well," she said reasonably. Molly couldn't have loved him very much if it was enough that another man looked at her and she dropped everything to run off with the other man.

"Believe me, he can."

"Pray, proceed. What happened next? I must confess, I am quite breathless with anticipation." Her fingers finally clenched around the hilt.

"She died."

Avery almost let go of the pistol. "That was rather abrupt. What exactly happened?"

"After an ill-fated expedition, the redcoats were on our backs, chasing us across the heath. We split up to make it harder for them to follow us. I rode back into the heath, while he, prize fool that he was, rode straight for the inn, the redcoats on his heels. There was shooting. Molly was caught in the crossfire. Dead."

Silence filled the carriage.

"I'm so sorry," she whispered.

"Aye, you should be. She died because of a criminal who thought he was better than others, who posed as a gentleman robber, when in fact he was no better than the rest of us. Scum of the earth. Needless to say, they caught me, clapped me in jail, and sentenced me to death while he escaped. He's been on the run ever since."

Avery digested the information.

Jerkins, a criminal?

Jerkins, a highwayman responsible for robbing hundreds of coaches? Maybe he'd even murdered.

A bitter taste crept into Avery's mouth. For the life of her, she could not picture Jerkins as a murderer.

But what did she really know about the man?

"It's a very sad story," she finally said. "But I fail to understand what I have to do with it. Why follow and kidnap me?"

"Word spread quickly after you walked into the Angel Inn like the naive, blue-eyed lamb that you are and asked for Jax Tyrrell. I had you followed, and you led me to a lovely townhouse in Wimpole Street, the butler of which looked very similar to my former accomplice who'd seemingly vanished from the face of the earth. While he was wallowing in wealth and luxury, rubbing shoulders with the pinks and the bucks, and fooling the aristocracy into thinking he was their servant, I was barely scraping by and didn't have a sixpence to my name. He still owes me some of the loot."

"You broke into the house."

"I had to make my presence known somehow." His white teeth gleamed in the dark. "Mind you, I did not take anything aside from his flask of terrible perfume."

"You did it deliberately to deceive me at Vauxhall. You wanted me to think you were him."

"Very clever, Lady Avery." He chuckled.

"Why?"

"One word: revenge."

Here it was, the crux of the matter. She licked her lips. "Revenge for what?"

"Simple. He took my woman. I take his."

"How very infantile."

"But effective." He looked out the window. "He'll be following us even as we speak." He opened the window and called the coachman to increase the speed.

She bumped around in the carriage as the horses raced down the road.

"Where are you taking me?"

"To a small hidden inn in the middle of the heath. He will know where it is. We will wait for him there. And I might hand you over. After I've had my way with you, of course."

Quick as a flash, he changed seats and sat down next to her, pushing her into the corner.

"I've already had a nice taste of you, and it has whetted my appetite for more. I must say, he always had good taste in women. Since I claim his ladybird as mine, you'll be the crown of my victory." He grabbed her by the chin and pulled her face up to press his mouth against hers.

But this time, Avery was prepared. She wriggled out of his grip, drove her elbow into his chest, and finally pulled out her pistol.

"Touch me again and you are dead." It would have sounded like a more ominous threat if her voice hadn't trembled.

He laughed.

Odious man!

"My gun is loaded. I warn you. I have practised shooting, and I am a sharp shot."

"The lady has spirit and claws. How sweet. Do you really think this toy in your hands can do anything?"

"It can blow huge holes in my cherry tree in the garden. I have had enough practice." She pulled back the hammer. "And Jerkins helped me."

He hesitated. "Has he, by Jove."

There was a slight uneasiness about him, and it encouraged her. "Tell the coachman to stop. Now."

The man raised his hands. "Very well. There will be a change of plans." He called the coachman to stop, and it came to a halt.

"Out." She waved the gun at the door. "Get out."

He hissed but did as she said.

Her plan had been to leave him stranded on the road while getting the coachman to take her back home. That she had miscalculated badly became clear to her in the next minute.

Before she could blink, he had pounced on her.

She fought like a wild cat, clawing, scratching, biting, and the pistol fell from her hand to the floor.

His hand covered her mouth, and she bit down on it, hard.

He swore in a string of colourful curses.

Then she kicked him below the belt, and he let go.

Avery fumbled for the gun, found it, pointed it at him, closed her eyes and fired.

There was silence at first. When Avery dared to open her eyes, he was standing in front of her, glaring.

Her stomach plummeted as she realised she'd missed.

"Are ye hurt, guv'nor?" A second figure appeared beside him, pointing a pistol at her. The coachman.

"She missed me by a hair's breadth." His hat lay on the ground with a hole in it. "Vixen."

Avery dropped the gun as it dawned on her she'd almost killed a man.

He was a horrid highwayman and probably deserved it if she had, especially with the way he'd treated her, but still. Now that she had no weapon to defend herself, he would probably kill her instead.

"Harridan. I must say, I prefer my women more docile and biddable."

"I didn't get the impression that Molly was such a docile and biddable woman," she replied with a raised chin. "And if you treated her the way you have just treated me, I dare say it was the best thing she could have done to leave you."

There. That sat.

In the moonlight illuminating the man's face, she could see that he was scowling. He had a narrow, gaunt face with dark eyes and thin lips and a scar running down his cheek.

"What do we do now, master?" the coachman asked. "If you ask me, we should just shoot her on the spot and get it over with."

Her captor looked at her thoughtfully. "No, John. That would be too easy. I want him to suffer a little. But I do have to admit I have lost my appetite, for the virago bites, and that is not to my taste. I prefer them soft and compliant. This one is sharp and has a tongue of acid. Get out."

He gave her a push, and Avery stumbled out of the carriage.

"Whatever you are up to, let me assure you, it will not succeed. My brother is a high-ranking diplomat, and the entire government will be on your trail until doomsday if you hurt as much as a hair on my head."

"I doubt it. Your brother has left the country and couldn't give a tuppence for his sister's welfare. I doubt he'd even scrape together a ransom to have you back."

His words were a cold slap across the face, and she took a step back. Truer words had never been spoken. Tears streamed into her eyes, and she clenched her fingers into fists.

She felt vulnerable, standing in the moonlit street with two fierce-looking criminals staring at her.

Her captor approached her, and she took a step back.

"Get back on, John," her captor bit out to the coachman over his shoulder. "We'll go on—alone. I want you to give him a message, so pay attention. Tell him I will meet him tomorrow night at the three linden trees to settle once and for all what he owes me. If he doesn't show up, I will take my revenge on you. I will be there in the shadows, following you; I will always know where you are, what you are doing, and I will leave my mark for you so you will never forget my presence, and you will never know where and when I will strike again."

He swung into the coach, and it set off before Avery could fully comprehend the meaning of his words.

Chapter Twenty-Five

THIS COULD NOT BE HAPPENING.

Avery stood alone by the side of the road, shivering as the wind tugged at her cloak with icy fingers. Her hair had come loose from its bun and was tumbling over her shoulders. To the left and right of the road was a thick copse of trees. There was no house in sight, no light anywhere, except for the moon, now uncooperative enough to hide behind the clouds.

There were two things she could do: collapse on the ground in a heap of misery and cry, or pull herself together and make her way back to London, hoping that along the way she would come across a house with friendly people who would take her in for the night and not rob her of her last penny. Not that she had anything of value with her; she'd left her bag in the carriage, and she'd lost the pistol.

The pistol!

She dropped to her knees to search for it, groping with her hands in the dark. When the moon finally decided to cooperate and emerged from behind the clouds, she found it lying by the side of the road. She picked it up, brushed it off, and clung to it as if her life depended on it, even though she'd used the only bullet it had and couldn't reload. Still, a pistol was a pistol, and clutching it to her chest gave her a strange sense of security.

Then she began to walk.

It was rather disconcerting to walk alone through one of the most perilous places in England, surrounded by nothing but dark shadows, the eerie hooting of owls, and the random cracking of twigs in the undergrowth. The ghostly whisper of the wind was the most frightening, and there were other sounds emerging from the depths of the heath that she dared not think about.

"Very well, Avery, you wanted an adventure. Behold, you are in the middle of one. Enjoy every minute of it, for any of this must be better than sitting in Great-Aunt Euphemia's parlour knitting blankets for the parish." Her voice trembled. The truth was, she would give anything right now to sit in Great-Aunt Euphemia's parlour, in front of a crackling fireplace, however small, and knit. It sounded positively heavenly to her. They would drink a pot of strong black tea with a dollop of milk. She could tell Great Aunt Euphemia her stories to pass the time. Even better if she was deaf and could not understand a word.

Goodness, what was that?

A black shadow broke from the treetops, swooped down, and passed close over her head, almost brushing her hair. She heard the flapping of wings, followed by a chittering, squeaking sound.

Avery screamed.

When she calmed down, she took a deep breath. "A bat. It was just a bat. Goodness gracious! How can such a small creature be so frightening? I really must regain my composure. This will not do. I will just have to tell myself my own stories to distract myself. Very well. The story of The Intrepid Highwayman. By Lady Avery Heywood. I really should think of a pseudonym, like Jerkins suggested." She sniffed. "I shall not think of Jerkins now because surely I'll burst into tears. Back to the highwayman. A lone highwayman galloped down the lonely road through the lone forest on his massive black steed, the moon lighting up his path to a sliver of silver. How very lonely he was, so entirely, completely on his own." She sniffed and wiped a hand over her cheeks. "The thundering hooves of his horse echoed eerily among the trees."

This was good. This was very, very good. So good, in fact, that she could even hear her own story. The galloping of hooves, a fast, thunderous rhythm, approached in the distance.

She tilted her head to one side and closed her eyes. "He galloped across the heather-covered moor. Wait. Jerkins said it wasn't possible, so he galloped along the road, of course, that endless, lonely road. Yes, he did. Getting closer and closer." Her teeth began to chatter. She stood petrified, listening to the galloping approach, until suddenly a massive black horse burst round the curve. She could see the steaming nostrils of the horse and heard it pant and neigh. Towering far above her, illuminated by the moonlight, was a dark, sinister rider.

The horse reared, the rider cursed, and with a muffled shriek, Avery fell backwards into a gorse bush.

After the rider had calmed his horse, she heard a rough voice above her say, "Stand up and give me your hand."

She scrambled up. "Begone highwayman, there is nothing to be gained here. Besides, I have a pistol." She clutched the barrel of her pistol and pointed the hilt at him.

His deep, rolling laugh made her skin crawl.

"Avery. Your hand. Unless you prefer to walk all the way back to London." He bent and held out his hand. "Give me your gun. I'll keep it for you. Let me help you to safety, and then we'll talk."

Avery peered at him suspiciously. He wore a mask, or perhaps it was the tricorn hat that shaded his eyes. His left hand held the bridle of the biggest horse she'd ever seen, and his right hand was outstretched towards her, waiting.

One should never get into strange carriages, she reminded herself. Look where that had led her. Neither should she get on a horse with a strange man, even if he did sound vaguely like Jerkins. And it was certainly the height of folly to surrender one's weapon to a highway robber. She decided it couldn't be helped. She handed over her pistol and watched as he tucked it away and held out his hand again. She grabbed his arm, and he pulled her up as easily as if she were a child, swinging her behind him. She sat astride, the skirt riding up, exposing her stockinged legs up to her thighs.

If Lady Jersey could see her now, she would undoubtedly revoke her Almack's voucher.

Avery would have fallen off the other side if she hadn't wrapped her hands around his waist and held on as if her life depended on it. Before she had the chance to settle, he'd given the horse the spurs and they were racing along the road.

She pressed her cheek against his back and felt his tense muscles against her. She inhaled his scent: leather and sweat and cologne. The only thought she was capable of was that she would hold on tight, for the rest of her life if necessary, and she would not let go. Not ever.

The wind bit into her cheeks, rushed past her ears, and drove tears into her eyes. The hood of her cloak was thrown back, revealing her hair flying behind her. The horse panted and its muscles moved beneath her. The rider in front of her rode like a man possessed, as if all the demons were after them.

After what seemed like an eternity, they came to a crossroads and took the path to the right, which led further into the thicket.

Avery had enough sense to know this was not the way she had come in the coach—this was not the way back to London.

After another hour of riding, her arms burning and legs chafed from the ride, she was convinced she would fall from the horse like a sack of flour when the thicket suddenly cleared into a wide alley framed by tall chestnut trees. They galloped straight towards a manor house that stood at the end of the avenue. She gaped at the massive, imposing structure, at least twice the size of Penmaron Hall. Proud and cold, the turrets reached far above the trees into the sky. As the horse galloped into the drive, lights appeared in the window, the door opened, and servants emerged with torches.

No sooner had the horse come to a halt than the rider swung down, turned to her, and lifted her off the horse, placing her on the ground in front of him. Her legs wobbled, and she collapsed against him as he held her up. He brushed strands of hair away from her gorse-scarred cheeks.

"Did he hurt you?" he bit out. His hands moved over her face, her head, her shoulders.

Unable to answer, she shook her head. "I'm fine. I fought him and almost shot him, and then he decided it was not worth going through with his plans, so he abandoned me in the middle of the road. He says he wants revenge, and you are to meet him tomorrow at the three linden trees, wherever that is."

"You brave, brave woman." He planted a hard kiss on her lips, and before she could realise what had just happened, he lifted her into his arms and carried her up the stairs to the house.

"We were not expecting you so late, my lord." A bewigged, bespectacled man in livery emerged from the main gate.

Jerkins. It shot through Avery's mind.

But no. This man wasn't Jerkins; he was smaller and thinner and older, and he spoke differently. Only the wig and spectacles were the same. And Jerkins was already with her, holding her in his arms as if she weighed nothing at all.

"Prepare a room and a bath and supper for the lady, and wake Fernsby if he's gone to bed."

"Mr Fernsby is still awake in the library, my lord."

"Excellent. Inform him of our arrival, but first see to Lady Avery's welfare."

"Of course, my lord."

He carried her into a massive hall panelled in dark oak, with a half-timbered ceiling and tall, stained-glass windows, almost cathedral-like.

"Where are we?" she asked. "And why are we here? Who is Fernsby?" She fought to be let down, but his grip on her tightened like bands of iron.

"Hush. Everything will be well."

She was tired and crabby, her muscles ached, and there was nothing she wanted more than a hot bath and a soft bed.

"You can let me down. I am not a child, and I want answers."

He ignored her request and carried her up a flight of stairs, taking them two at a time, entering a room so exquisite that Avery forgot her bad mood. He lowered her gently onto a four-poster bed.

"Promise me you will stay here and have a bath and supper and then sleep and not run away again?" He gently brushed a strand of hair from her face and tucked it behind her ear. "Those scratches need looking after, and you have dark rings under your eyes."

"Not until you tell me where I am," she insisted.

"At Thornwood Hall."

"Thornwood Hall. I have never heard of it. Who lives here?"

"Thornwood Hall is my home."

This massive gothic castle was his home?

Avery rubbed her forehead wearily. "I don't understand anything anymore."

"I promise you answers will be forthcoming."

"You always say that," she grumbled. "I refuse to be sent to bed like a child. I want to talk. Now."

"Very well. First a bath, then supper, then we will talk."

At that moment, the maids came in with buckets of steaming water, and there was nothing she wanted more than to step into the copper tub draped with linen they had set up and soothe her tired muscles.

He planted a kiss on her forehead and left.

After Avery had bathed, the maid pulled a blue damask gown over her head, placed slippers on her feet, and combed her hair. She dabbed ointment on all her cuts and bruises, and served her a tray of food, which she gobbled down hungrily.

"What's your master's name?" she asked the maid, who came to ask if she wanted more tea.

"Lord Julius Blackshurst, my lady."

"I mean the man who just carried me into this room."

"Yes, my lady. It is Blackshurst."

Ah. Well. She supposed she shouldn't be surprised that Jerkins had always been Blackshurst in reality. So the identity he'd been impersonating all along was that of the butler. She felt a pang of sadness at that, for she'd grown rather fond of Jerkins the butler.

Blackshurst, on the other hand...a range of emotions swept through her: confusion, annoyance, wariness...excitement?

She shook her head to sweep those feelings away.

"I thought Lord Blackshurst was abroad," she replied with a frown.

"Yes, my lady, his lordship has been travelling extensively on the continent, but he recently returned."

"How recently?"

"He returned a few weeks ago, my lady."

None of this made any sense. Jerkins, or Blackshurst, had never left, so how he could have returned was a mystery to her. Unless, of course, he was just pretending to have left, keeping even his servants in the dark.

Avery rubbed her aching head.

"Is he a good master?"

"Yes, my lady. The best there ever was," the girl replied promptly.

"And who is Mr Fernsby?"

"Mr Benjamin Fernsby is his lordship's godfather."

Avery digested this as she finished her tea and ate the last morsel of bread. She pushed the tray away, and the maid took it from the room.

"'The gentlemen are waiting for you in the library, my lady."

She dismissed the maid, telling her she would find her own way to the library. She needed a few minutes to gather her thoughts and to come up with an appropriate response to this turn of events. She followed the path back down the massive oak staircase, studying the oil portraits hanging on the wall, mostly landscapes and hunting scenes. As she approached the half-open door on the right-hand side of the hall, following the maid's directions, she heard two angry male voices shouting at each other.

Her hand, which had reached out to push the door open, froze.

"Have you completely lost your mind? If you go after him, it will all have been for nothing! I won't allow it! I did not invest a fortune for you to go straight back to the gallows!" A rusty, unfamiliar male voice shouted.

"Curse it, Ben, don't you understand? He will never stop unless he's eliminated!" That was Blackshurst's voice shouting back.

"Yes, and to what end? And at what cost? If it all blows up, this time no fortune in the world will be able to save you."

"It won't blow up. I'll see to it," Blackshurst snarled.

"Are you really prepared to throw away everything you have so painstakingly built up over the last few years? Can't you see that's exactly what he wants? He's baiting you, using this woman, and you're falling head over heels for it."

"He wants revenge, and he will not stop until he gets it. Next time he'll use even cruder methods, and he won't stop at just kidnapping her. He has already hurt her. He's a dead man, and he knows it."

Avery shuddered at his cold voice.

"Curse it, Jax! Women have always been your downfall. I won't have it!"

She gasped and put her hands over her mouth, but it

was too late. The two men had heard her, and the room was suddenly silent.

She heard footsteps approaching, and the door opened.

"Come in, Lady Avery," Blackshurst said in a weary voice.

Chapter Twenty-Six

AVERY GAPED AT HIM.

He'd taken off his coat, and his shirt sleeves were up to his elbows, revealing powerful arms. He wore black leather breeches and riding boots, and his dark hair fell over his forehead. He beckoned her into the room.

A fire was roaring in the fireplace, and in front of it a man sat hunched over in a chair with wheels, his legs covered by a plaid blanket. The man studied her with sharp, piercing eyes before saying, "You'll have to excuse me for not getting up. My sorry legs," he patted them, "have proven quite useless since I was born, and they are not improving as I get older. So, you're Lady Avery." He made a slight bow.

"This obstinate old man is Mr Benjamin Fernsby," Blackshurst grumbled. "My godfather."

"How do you do, sir." She stood in front of him and wrung her hands.

"As you have no doubt overheard my godson bellow, he is about to throw himself into an impetuous and foolhardy exploit, hence my displeasure which I may have voiced with equally excessive—but very necessary —force."

"Ben," Blackshurst warned.

Fernsby raised his hand to silence him. "But before we get into all that, let me enquire how you are after your harrowing experience. It must have been very frightening." He motioned for her to sit in the chair beside him. "Pray, sit while you tell your story."

Avery glanced at the thunderous face of Blackshurst as he took up his position by the fireplace before she sat down. Since the two men looked at her expectantly, she began to tell them in a halting voice how she had received the letter, how she had decided to meet the mysterious sender—Blackshurst's face darkened even more—how she had arrived at the inn and how she'd been forced into the carriage. How she hadn't been able to identify the man who had told her a strangely romantic tale, dripping with pathos, of her butler, highwaymen, a tragic love triangle, and revenge. How he'd seemed reasonable and strangely polite up to that point, and how his behaviour had suddenly become threatening and sinister. How he'd outed himself as Jax Tyrrell.

"A pernicious lie," Fernsby interjected. "He only did so because his own name, Syd Barker, has fallen into obscurity. Easier to steal the name of a legend."

She continued to relate how she'd fought and defended herself with her pistol—Blackshurst growled— at which point her kidnapper must have decided she wasn't worth the trouble and left her on the road in the middle of the night with a message for Blackshurst.

"Or Jerkins. Or Jax." She threw up her hands. "Whoever you are! I no longer know who he could have meant, because I am quite upset and annoyed by this whole situation, and especially by you!" She threw an angry glance at Blackshurst, who scowled back at her with crossed arms. "Will you finally explain your identity, sir?"

"The lady's right, Jax. You do owe her an explanation," Fernsby said. "After all, it's because of you that she was kidnapped by this man."

"His name is Syd. Syd Barker. He's a dastardly scoundrel, a low thief and a highwayman, and he deserves to die." He ground out the words.

"I've established that much," Avery replied, "and while all that is certainly interesting, what I want to know is about you, not him. Especially if your godfather happened to call you 'Jax' after you denied it when I confronted you about it in no uncertain terms earlier."

"Did you, by Jove?" Fernsby lifted his eyebrows in amusement. "That's exceedingly clever of you. Knowing Jax, he denied it, of course. But I see this conversation is getting us nowhere. I will take the lead and tell Lady Avery your whole sorry story, if you insist on beating around the bush."

Blackshurst shrugged.

"The man you see sulking there was born Julius Alexander Jerkins Cawthorne. He called himself Jax when he could barely speak, so the name stuck in the nursery."

"Julius Alexander Jerkins," Avery whispered. "Jax."

"The name Tyrrell comes from his mother's side. Jax became the thirty-eighth Earl of Blackshurst at the tender age of ten after his parents were tragically killed in an accident."

"Oh!" Her hands fluttered to her neck. "Such a sad beginning."

"Hardly an accident," Blackshurst growled.

"An accident," Fernsby repeated firmly. "An accident, however, that was to have serious repercussions on this boy's life. You may have heard of the Gordon Riots, when the mob overran the streets, looting and burning chapels, embassies, and even my bank. When the army was called in to quell the riots, the violence reached its peak. Jax's parents happened to be in the wrong place at the wrong time and were caught in the crossfire. The sound of musketry sent the horses running, and their carriage plunged over the bridge. After their tragic deaths, I stepped in as a father figure. I did a terrible job of it too, spoiling him too much, heaven forgive me, but I meant well." He paused and peered at Blackshurst, a flicker of fondness in his eyes.

"I can see now that I should have walloped him regularly; instead, I tried to be understanding of the troubled little orphan that he was. Jax grew up restless and bored, no doubt due to the excessive privileges he had been given too much and too early. A title, a castle, riches, every wish read from his eyes and too much freedom. It is enough to spoil any child."

Blackshurst scoffed, but once more Fernsby raised his hand. "Jax grew resentful of authority of any kind, and he developed a particular dislike for redcoats. His aim in life was one thing and one thing only: to bend the law and make it his own. It became a sport in his life to challenge the law and then escape the consequences by a hair's breadth. He once almost burned down this very house in an attempt to imitate Guy Fawkes."

"An experiment with fireworks that went wrong," Blackshurst explained.

"Then he fell in with a bad lot and befriended all sorts of horrible people, drunkards, pickpockets, and criminals."

"My nanny taught me to love all people equally, regardless of their backgrounds," Blackshurst replied with a raised eyebrow.

"Nonsense. You gave that poor woman grey hairs with your wild ways. And it was almost impossible to keep a tutor. We must have gone through nearly twenty before I gave up. The final one lasted no more than ten minutes."

Blackshurst shrugged. "He objected to me calling him a muttonhead when he did not know the answer to my question as to how many barrels of explosives it would take to blow up London Bridge. I was an inquisitive boy, you see."

"He was, in short, an *enfant terrible* in the truest sense of the word. A veritable spawn of the devil, beyond redemption." Fernsby shook his head sadly.

"I can certainly imagine that," Avery replied with an unsteady voice.

Fernsby cast a brooding glance at Blackshurst. "I can't remember when a boy's mischievous prank turned into crime. When did those little pickpocketing tricks he'd learned from one of his 'friends', in which he relieved a person of their purse or pocket-watch, turn into a taste for full-blown highway robbery? I really cannot say."

To this, Blackshurst offered no comment.

There was silence in the room, aside from the crackling of the fire.

"I confess, I blame myself," Fernsby went on. "It was at a time when I was too occupied with the affairs of my banks, and I had little time for the boy. Of course, I brought him lavish gifts, a stallion, then a curricle, but none of these could replace what the boy needed most."

"And what do you think that would have been?" Blackshurst asked with a sneer.

"Simple." Avery clasped her hands in her lap. "A mother, of course."

Blackshurst's sneer died on his face, replaced with a haunted look. "Or a spinster aunt to tuck me into bed and tell me wonderful stories. I dare say that the devil's spawn might well have turned out differently had there been such a person in his life." The look he gave her burned into her soul. "Are you even aware of how lucky your nephews are to have had you in their lives?"

Suddenly she had a lump in her throat. She looked away.

Fernsby nodded. "Yes. You are quite right, Lady Avery. So, unable to provide him with what he needed most, I was all too willing to be blind to his faults and let him run wild. Little did I know that behind all the tales spreading like wildfire across the countryside of a new legendary highwayman, more famous than Dick Turpin and Claude DuVall combined, was my boy, who had donned a highwayman's mask, joined a gang, and robbed the very people he'd been entertaining in this very house just an hour before. Oh, the lark! Of course, when the name Jax Tyrrell became famous, there was no doubt in my mind who it could be." He shook his head sadly.

"But wouldn't his name have given him away? Wouldn't people have recognised him?" Avery asked.

Fernsby shook his head. "Jax was what he'd called himself since he was a child, but only I, his mother, and his nanny ever called him that. The rest of the staff here, if they ever knew, kept mum, and will until the day they die, for they are loyal to Blackshurst and would never breathe a word against their master. To this very day I keep wondering what must have gone through that addled brain of his."

"I was bored and thought it amusing." Blackshurst studied his fingernails.

Avery stared at him. "You thought robbing people was amusing?"

"For a while, I suppose. They were all drunk, I made sure of that when they were here at one of my drinking parties. And afterwards I would relieve them of their baubles and purses." He shrugged. "It was a game. They never knew who I was. I never hurt any of them. Most of the time my pistol was unloaded. I thought it was a great joke to teach them a little lesson. I'd give back the loot afterwards, throw it back through the window or hand it to the coachman, so no real harm was done."

"Until you finally achieved what you wanted, and the redcoats were at your heels."

"They were unable to catch me. Nobody knows the heath as well as I do. And occasionally, when I did keep a purse, which was not often, I threw it to those who needed it more."

"Oh, so now you think that highway robbery was a true act of charity, in the service of the common good. Like Robin Hood. Taking from the rich and giving to the poor." Her voice dripped with sarcasm.

"I certainly used to see it in that light. Syd Barker was different; he always kept his loot. We used to have furious arguments over it."

"Why did it never occur to you to just take your own wealth, of which you had plenty, and give it away? Start a charity. The Blackshurst Foundation." She waved her hand. "Since you hardly knew what to do with your riches and were so bored with it all."

Blackshurst stared into the crackling fire, as if searching for the answer there. "But, Lady Avery, what would be the fun in that? It was the thrill, the excitement, the chase that I lived for."

Fernsby nodded in agreement. "Breaking the law and then escaping it was what heated his blood. It was almost an addiction. Especially if he could get one over on the redcoats who were only doing their duty. It all stems from a deep-seated hatred of them. Because you blame them for the death of your parents."

Blackshurst walked over to a side table and poured himself a glass of whisky. His hand was not quite steady as he poured it down his throat.

"I'll have one too, if you please," she heard herself say.

Blackshurst curled his lips into a smile and handed her a glass, and another to Fernsby. "To Benjamin

Fernsby. A true hero for having raised this devil's spawn." He raised his glass in a mocking toast.

Avery downed her glass of whisky, choking as the liquid burned her throat. She set the glass down. "Go on. Tell me the story of Molly."

"Ah, Molly. Beautiful, dark-eyed Molly." He stared morosely into his empty glass, as if he regretted drinking it.

Another pang of jealousy shot through her. She quenched it.

"A victim of circumstances." Fernsby lifted his glass, and Blackshurst refilled it.

"'This Syd Barker said she was his bride and that you stole her from him," she prompted.

A brief look of sadness crossed his face. "Yes."

The answer threw her. She'd expected a denial or a change of story, not a confirmation.

"It's true. They were to be married, and I could not resist taking her away from him. Just to see if I could, and if she would go with me, you know."

Fernsby shook his grey head back and forth, sadly. "He's a terrible womaniser. See that beam over there?" He pointed to a black beam in the ceiling that hung lower than the others. "If you walk up to it, you can see etchings in it."

Avery stood up and inspected the beam. It was indeed full of lines etched into the wood.

She stared at them in disbelief.

"I gave up counting long ago," said Fernsby. "How many are there?"

Blackshurst shrugged.

"Good heavens. An etching for every woman you've seduced?" She had finally found her voice.

He looked sheepish. "Most of them were the follies of my youth."

"And Molly was one of them." She sat down. "Tell me the story."

Chapter Twenty-Seven

BLACKSHURST PACED THE ROOM. THE FIRE THREW shadows over him, making the angles in his face—the cheekbones, the eagle nose, and the high forehead—appear sharper, starker than in daylight. "It was merely a prank, a test, as it were. At least at first. To see if she really loved Syd as much as she said she did. But I suspected she really preferred the blunt and the baubles he'd brought her, and I noticed her eyes wandering to me all too often at the inn. I encouraged her. I flirted with her. It was easy to turn her head. As soon as she did, I lost interest in her. Who wants an unfaithful woman? But she became obsessed. One night she followed me and told me I had pretty manners and that she wanted a gentleman because Syd was low-born and not gentleman enough for her." He sneered. "I gave her a kiss and sent her back to Syd. She took it badly."

"You can hardly blame her," Avery said dryly. "You played with her. She must have been very angry."

"Quite. She raged and ranted. Said she would get

227

even with me. I laughed it off at the time. But she was true to her word." He stopped pacing and stared at the toes of his boots. "She informed the redcoats of our next exploit. Syd always talked too much when he was drunk, and he must have given her some of the information. Or, more likely, she'd wormed it out of him. So, the very next night, they ambushed us. Syd managed to escape, and I tried to follow. We would have got away if Molly hadn't suddenly appeared on a horse and thrown herself into the fray. God only knows what the woman was doing there; maybe she'd changed her mind at the last minute and wanted to save Syd. She was caught in the crossfire and shot by one of the soldiers."

His jaw was set. "Syd got away, but they captured me when I tried to retrieve Molly's body."

"As tragic as all this is, you must appreciate the irony," Fernsby chimed in. "In the end it was a woman who was responsible for Jax Tyrrell's downfall."

"How old were you when all this happened?" Avery inquired.

"Twenty."

"And how old were you when you first started your career as a highway robber?"

"Sixteen."

"Sixteen!" She clapped her hands together. "Good heavens! You were barely three years older than my eldest nephew."

"Indeed. Young, foolish beyond words, but certainly not innocent." Fernsby tugged at the blanket covering his lap. "The best thing that could have happened to that wild cub was to get arrested on charges of highway robbery and to get a taste of gaol. I always had a suspicion that, underneath it all, that was what he wanted: to be finally caught."

"Far from it. A fortnight in Newgate certainly cured me of any criminal ambitions." Blackshurst raked a hand through his hair. "Wouldn't wish it on my worst enemy. It was a miracle I survived and didn't die of one of the many diseases that circulated in those noxious dungeons."

Avery blinked at him, bewildered. "But I don't understand. There must have been a trial. It must have been in the papers. They must have discovered your true identity and then you were sent to the gallows and hanged. It was said to have been a huge event, almost a festival. A huge procession from Newgate to Tyburn. Jax Tyrrell is dead. I have seen his gravestone."

Fernsby nodded. "Yes, that is the story we have painstakingly put together. It is what the public believes, and it has become a beloved legend that we do not want to unravel, even though Jax is trying his best to do so at the moment." He glared at Blackshurst. Turning to Avery, he said, "I have my connections too, you know."

"How so?"

Blackshurst leaned against the mantelpiece with his arms crossed. "Benjamin here has been governor of the Bank of England for decades. After the Prince Regent and Lord Liverpool, our Prime Minister, he is said to be the third most powerful man in England."

Fernsby folded his hands in prayer position and placed them against his lips. After a while, he said, "Then there is the matter of Blackshurst being a peer. One does not condemn earls to the death of common criminals.

The Chief Justice, who happened to be a good friend of mine, had no interest in hanging him, but he did want to teach Jax a lesson by letting him languish in Newgate for a while. Oh yes, there was a trial, mind you, because justice had to be done, and there was nothing I could do about it, nor would I have wanted to. Thanks to my influence and a hefty bribe, he not only escaped the gallows, but we managed to keep the actual trial out of the public eye. I moved heaven and earth to keep his identity a secret. There is no connection between Blackshurst and Jax Tyrrell. I made sure of that. But although Jax had committed highway robbery, a crime punishable by death, he had returned the stolen goods in one way or another. What saved him was a notebook in which he meticulously recorded all the loot he'd stolen and then returned. It was possible to trace every stolen item back to its owner, who all confirmed that they had been returned. Jax was reprimanded and released on the condition that he mend his ways."

Avery blinked in confusion. "But who was hanged at Tyburn?"

"A poor devil who was sentenced to death and bribed to go to the gallows in the name of Jax Tyrrell. He was going to hang anyway. He could die the ignoble death of a common criminal, or he could die under the name of the legendary highwayman, be served an elaborate last supper, and die knowing his widow and children would be provided for for the rest of their lives. He willingly went along with the plan."

"You've seen the gravestone," Blackshurst said. "The man who lies in that grave is John Wiles, common horse thief." There was a grim expression on his face. "We spoke in gaol. He was otherwise a simple, decent man. His main crime was trying to feed his family, and he had the misfortune to be caught on his first ill-fated attempt to steal a horse." He pulled himself up. "That's the difference, you see. Noblemen can get away with almost anything, as I am a prime example, but if you're a starving peasant trying to feed your family, they'll hang you. That is the justice of our land." A muscle twitched in his cheek.

"It almost sounds like you were disappointed that they didn't hang you." Avery tilted her head inquisitively to one side.

Fernsby slapped his hands on the armrest. "That's what I keep saying: this boy has a death wish."

"And what happened to the widow and the children?"

Blackshurst pulled up one corner of his lips. "Who do you think your abigail Emma is?"

Her eyes widened. "No. His widow?"

"His eldest daughter."

"Hetty Wiles," she breathed. "Stabbing Hetty. So it was true she was in gaol for being a murderess?"

"We found her in gaol for attempted murder, yes. She worked as an abigail for the Duchess of Thistlethorpe. She defended herself when the son of the household attempted to rape her. We managed to clear her name and get her out. We'd promised it to Wiles, after all."

Avery digested this. "And that new footman you hired. Fred. I assume he must be his son, no doubt."

Blackshurst nodded. "He worked here at Thornwood Hall for a while, until I decided I needed additional staff in my townhouse." He looked at her steadily. "An occupant unexpectedly decided to prolong her stay, you see, so I needed more domestics. Mrs Wiles is the housekeeper here now. I believe she served you dinner in your room earlier."

Avery remembered a quiet but dignified woman who'd served her dinner tray earlier. So she was the widow of the man who hung as Jax Tyrrell.

"And Belinda?" she gasped.

Blackshurst shook his head. "No, she really is one of your relatives. Slightly impoverished, but happy to be her cousin's new companion so she can pay off her extensive gambling debts."

"And Jerkins?" Inexplicably, her heart began to pound.

"After that fiasco, Jax had to disappear for at least a decade or two," Fernsby interjected. "Blackshurst travelled on the continent until the wars broke out but decided it best not to return just yet under his real name. But return to London he did."

"But with the legend of Jax Tyrrell at an end, you decided to become a butler," Avery said quietly. "What better way to hide from the face of society than to live in its midst. My brother never suspected who you were, did he?"

"It was Fernsby's idea. It allowed me to be in London without drawing attention to myself. Being a butler in the Fothergill household was no challenge for a few months a year during the Season. Lord and Lady Fothergill were away most of the time and oblivious to household matters. I could be gone for hours on end, and no one would notice. And you were too busy with the children to notice my frequent absences. I could do a Season and play butler to Fothergill, I told myself." Blackshurst clasped his hands behind his back. "It would cement my identity as a butler."

"He ended up doing three, for no reason at all." Fernsby gave Blackshurst a wry look.

Blackshurst ran his hand through his hair and looked away.

Fernsby smirked. "One day Jax came to me and insisted that Blackshurst was not ready to return from his travels and that he needed to extend his role as butler for another Season. It took me some digging to discover that the reason was, as always, a woman." He threw up his hands.

"Only this time it was rather odd, I must say. Turned out the blighter had fallen deeply and desperately in love with the little lady there and refused to let up the rent to be near her." Fernsby shook his head in exasperation. "Said she had no idea he even existed, and even though they saw each other every day, she could not see him as anything other than a butler. Said he couldn't leave her alone yet; that he had to watch over her, which caused him all sorts of headaches and troubles, which, I dare say, he deserved."

"Fernsby!" Blackshurst snapped. "Enough!" A dull red had crept up his neck.

"What? Who? Surely not Selena." Avery blinked at him in confusion. Then, as his words sank in and realisation dawned, a hot wave of red flushed her entire body. "Oh!"

Fernsby chuckled. "Ah, but that is no longer my story. I must say, it is getting rather late, and these old bones of mine are getting weary. I shall retire." Somehow, he'd turned his chair towards her. "Lady Avery, talk some sense into him, I beg you. Don't let all this end in tragedy." He rang a bell and a tall footman entered and pushed the chair out of the room.

Avery was left alone in the room with Blackshurst, who had sat down on the other side of the sofa and was staring at his steepled fingers as if they were the most fascinating thing in the room.

"Ignore him. My godfather is a meddlesome old man."

"Oh. Then it's not true?" She felt like bursting into tears. She should have swallowed her tongue. But the bitter disappointment that had settled like a millstone in the pit of her stomach at his suddenly withdrawn, cold demeanour had prompted those words. She could not explain the upheaval inside her, the intense embarrassment, then the intense joy, followed by the uncontrollable urge to cry.

She swallowed it all and bravely lifted her chin.

He rubbed his hands over his thighs. "Benjamin is a hopeless romantic underneath all his sarcasm. There is nothing he wants more than to see me leg-shackled and living the conventional life with a wife and child." He gave a curt laugh. "As if that were ever possible."

"Why is it so impossible?"

Blackshurst jumped to his feet again, spun around the room, stopped in front of a chair, and dug his fingers into its back.

"I have no time for a wife and child. They would be a

234

liability, forever in danger. Because of me. I couldn't imagine living a life in fear for their welfare. And then there is me, of course," he laughed bitterly. "A former criminal with a shady past, a life with a double, triple identity. I am no good. I have nothing to offer, nothing..."

Avery jumped to her feet, crossed the room in two, three strides and put her hands on his lips. "Shhh." She stood on tiptoe, pulled her fingers away, and pressed her lips to his for a sweet, lingering kiss.

A sound escaped his throat, his hand came up to cradle her neck, and he kissed her like a man drowning.

Then he drew her to the sofa and settled her on his lap, burying his head in her hair.

"Avery. Avery. What are we to do?" It sounded like a cry for help.

"Tell each other the truth, for one." She took his face in her hands and looked deep into his eyes. She traced his eyebrows and high cheekbones with the tips of her fingers, touched his long lashes in wonder, and the delicate curve of his lips.

He caught her fingers between his and nipped gently.

She shivered.

"I want to know if what Fernsby said was true," she said quietly. "About you only staying in the household because of m-me."

Panic flashed in his smoky grey eyes, eyes she'd grown to love since the day she thought she was leaving Wimpole Street forever. "There were all sorts of reasons why I stayed. Suffice it to say, there is no need for change. Let us go on as before. I will be your butler and take care of you."

"That isn't good enough for me." She dropped her hands.

He leaned his forehead against hers and closed his eyes. "I know," he whispered. "And yet, you are not to be one of those etchings on the beam, either."

"Not even if I wanted to?" Her voice sounded thick.

"Not even then," he said sadly.

"What happens now?"

His hands dropped to her waist as he set her down from his lap.

"You are tired and need to rest. As for me, I have some business to attend to."

The way he said it made her look up sharply. "You want to go after Syd Barker tonight. You never intended to meet him at the three lindens, as he requested. You will have your personal revenge tonight." Nausea rose inside her.

He did not answer but retreated once more behind his hard shell.

"That's what Fernsby meant, didn't he?" she pressed. A sense of foreboding filled her. "It will be a tragedy if you go."

Blackshurst looked at her wearily. "There will be an even bigger tragedy if I don't."

"I think Fernsby is right. You must let it go. You can't undo the past, and if you tug at even one thread, the entire thing will unravel."

"If I do nothing, the past will come and claim not only me, but Fernsby and you and so many other people who have come to rely on me. That is a risk I cannot take. This must be done once and for all, and only in this way can the past be laid to rest. Can you trust me?"

Avery stood in the middle of the room, biting her lower lip and shaking her head. "I don't want you to go."

"You have to trust me."

"Please don't go."

"Avery."

But she'd turned away, her heart heavy with foreboding. She stumbled out of the room, not wanting him to see the tears streaming down her face.

Chapter Twenty-Eight

AVERY DID NOT SLEPT ALL NIGHT.

She'd heard voices in the courtyard, and when she'd looked through her bedroom window in the light of the torches, she'd seen the black horse and a black figure galloping down the alley and disappearing in the darkness.

She'd huddled in her bed all night, face drawn and eyes burning, unable to sleep, waiting for the sound of the horse's hooves to return.

Trust me, he'd said.

She found she could not.

Blackshurst, who was Jerkins, who was Jax. Who was he, really?

Could it be true, as Fernsby had said, that he'd stayed in Wimpole Street only because of her? Because he loved her?

It would give her no peace.

She got up, dressed, and found her way to the breakfast room. She hadn't expected Fernsby to be up so early at barely five in the morning, but here he was, sitting at the table, eating kippers with calmness as if nothing in the world could shake him.

"Good morning." She felt suddenly shy.

"Lady Avery." He put down his cutlery and peered at her over his spectacles.

"Blackshurst hasn't returned yet?" It was an obvious question.

He closed his eyes for a moment. "He hasn't. Nor is he likely to any time soon. Come, please. Join me and let us pass the time in conversation. It's not every day I get to enjoy the company of a beautiful woman alone, without Jax constantly monopolising her attention."

Avery smiled involuntarily and sat down.

He gave her a long look. "Judging by your pale cheeks and dark rings under your eyes, you didn't sleep well either."

She shook her head. "I couldn't. I'm sorry I couldn't keep him away from his 'business,' as he called it. He asked me to trust him." She picked up a silver fork and absently touched the prongs with her fingertips. "I'm inclined not to, however."

Fernsby nodded. He leaned his elbows on the table, brought his palms together, and touched them to his mouth as he watched her. "With everything you heard last night, you are wondering what to make of it all. What is the truth? Can anyone's word be trusted in this house? Can any of it be believed?" He leaned back in his chair. "And it is good to ask these questions. It is wise not to take any story for granted. I can only say that whatever folly Jax committed in his youth, he paid dearly for it. He went to Newgate a foolish boy and came out a sober man. I was afraid they'd break him, but his spirit was strong enough to withstand whatever they did to him there. I would never have believed it, but he seemed to truly enjoy his work as a butler in your household. Then, when the time came for Blackshurst to return and take his place in society, I was surprised he resisted. I now understand it was because you chose to remain in the house. Would you like to tell me your side of the story?"

Avery did. When she had finished, she added, "I take full responsibility for these past events. If I hadn't insisted on meeting Syd Barker at the inn—which in retrospect was such a half-witted thing to do, my only excuse is that I was not thinking at all—much of what has happened in the last few days could have been avoided. And now Jerkins—Blackshurst—Jax—"

"You could just call him Julius," Fernsby put in unhelpfully.

"Another name to confuse me even more? Certainly not." She glared at him. "What was I saying? Oh, yes. Now, thanks to my foolishness, he has gone off to meet that awful man." She rubbed her forehead. "Has there been any news?"

Fernsby sighed. "I'm afraid not. We shall have to wait, as usual. It's the story of my life. The boy storms off on some adventure or other and the rest of us stay behind, twiddle our thumbs, and pray the worst doesn't come to pass. Although you could argue that it has, and that it can hardly get any worse."

Avery licked her lips nervously. "What do you suppose could happen?"

"Other than killing Syd, or getting himself killed, or arrested, and having his whole history unravelling and being revealed? I do not believe for a moment that they will send him to the gallows, but if the story gets out, it would be a public execution of the Blackshurst name. Not that there's much left to kill," he added dryly, "as he's done his best to live up to the name of 'The Black Earl.' " He looked up at her, a wry look in his eyes. "Though I have to say, he's changed since he met you. He may finally be ready to leave his wild ways behind and settle down for good. It would certainly be about time."

She shook her head. "I think you are mistaken, sir. He told me the opposite."

Fernsby snorted. "The man has the courage of ten lions when it comes to facing an entire army, but when it comes to confessing the truth in his heart, he is reduced to a simpering coward. He has spoken of only you these past years, from the time you knew him as a mere butler in the household. I have never seen him make such a cake of himself over a woman, yet there is no greater coward when it comes to admitting his feelings. He would rather worship you while hiding in another identity than honestly reveal what's in his heart."

Surely none of his words could be true. Avery felt herself flush hotly, and she was about to retort that he must be wrong about everything he'd just said, when there was the sound of swiftly approaching footsteps in the hallway. The door to the dining room was flung open, and a footman rushed in.

"Sir, there is news," he gasped. "There's terrible, terrible news."

"Out with it, boy, no dithering. What has happened?" Fernsby gripped the armrests of his chair until his knuckles whitened. Something tight and ugly coiled around Avery's heart.

"They say there was a shooting on the heath. His lordship was chasing the criminal Syd Barker."

"And?" Fernsby barked.

The footman closed his eyes for a moment before saying, "Dead."

"Syd Barker. That was to be expected."

There was a bleak look in the footman's eyes as he whispered, "No, sir, both of them."

Chapter Twenty-Nine

AVERY FELT ALL THE BLOOD AND WARMTH IN HER body sucked out of her as the whole world tilted. She gripped the edge of the table.

Fernsby moaned like a wounded animal.

Struggling for composure, Avery said, "Where? Where is his b-body?"

"At the inn, my lady," the footman said unhappily. "Sir, you must go there to identify the bodies."

With an iron will, Avery pulled herself to her feet. "Yes. You must go. I will go with you. I refuse to believe a word until I've seen the body myself."

Fernsby had shrunk into his chair and seemed half the size he once was. He looked up with difficulty. "You are right, Lady Avery. Let us not believe the worst until we have seen it with our own eyes." His hand shook as he brushed a strand of grey hair from his forehead. "But this is no mission for a lady. You must not accompany me on this terrible task."

"Nonsense." She was already halfway out of the room, fetching a cloak. "Let us go at once."

The journey to the inn was torture. Fernsby sat hunched over in a corner, next to the footman who'd carried him from the house to the carriage. His wheelchair was attached to the back of it.

Avery was in shock, her mind unable to move beyond the words, *He's dead, he's dead, he's dead,* followed by an even more vicious voice, *and it's your fault.*

If he really was dead, he'd gone before she could tell him she loved him.

Yes. She loved him.

When had she realised that?

She'd loved him since he'd carried her up the stairs that night when she'd decided to return to Wimpole Street. Or maybe even before that, she suspected, when she'd said goodbye to him for the first time that fateful day and realised Jerkins existed beyond his role as butler. He'd watched over her with gentle care, reading every wish from her eyes before she could even utter it. He knew her like no other person in the world. He knew her likes and dislikes, she'd shared her wishes and dreams with him, even her stories, fantastical as they were. He'd gone out of his way to help her make some of her dreams come true.

He'd taken on the role of Blackshurst so she could have a dance partner; only, of course, he had been Blackshurst all along, so there hadn't been too much pretence.

Blackshurst had swept her off her feet, and while she'd loved Jerkins, she'd fallen for Blackshurst with a passion she'd never thought possible.

And then there was Jax Tyrrell, a shadow of the younger man he'd once been, a lovable rogue, more legend than reality, the hero of her stories.

All three fused into one person.

All three lost to her own folly.

A lone tear finally rolled down her cheek, and she wiped it away with her hand.

As the carriage rolled through the desolate landscape, Avery made a vow. If he was dead, she would spend the rest of her life wearing black, mourning a love that was never to be. If he lived—and oh, how she prayed he did!—she would put an end to her foolish exploits and burn her 'Never List.' She would go to Dorset to look after Great-Aunt Euphemia and learn to live contentedly in the country. This she vowed to do.

There was a great deal of activity outside the inn, which was teeming with horses, carriages, people, and soldiers.

Avery and Fernsby were led to a dank room on the upper floor.

Two beds stood in the room, one against each wall, with bodies under a blanket.

"Put me down," Fernsby said to his man, "and bring my chair." The footman set up his wheelchair and gently placed him in it. Fernsby waved him away.

"Go," he ordered.

She began to tremble as her eyes fell on the outlines of the bodies on the beds.

"The moment of truth has arrived, Lady Avery. But I fear I lack the courage." Fernsby's voice trembled. "This boy has meant more to me than my own flesh. I loved him more than my own soul."

Avery's breath shook. "Let us not speak in the past tense yet." She walked briskly to the right side of the bed, held out a hand, and threw back the covers.

The face that stared back at her was pale, haggard, and the eyes that stared back at her sightlessly were...

"...not grey." Her voice trembled. "Syd Barker. He is indeed dead."

She turned to the other bed in horror. The bile rose in her throat, and her hand shook violently as she carefully pulled back the covers.

There was a roaring in her ears so loud that she could not hear Fernsby's pitiful moan. He had to repeat three times, "For heaven's sake, tell me what you see!" And when she did not respond, he rolled his wheelchair beside her and pulled the blanket away.

"Dear sweet heavens," he gasped, as he gazed down at a ginger-haired man with a rugged beard. "Who on earth is that?"

"It's not him." Avery's legs finally gave way under her, and she fell to the floor beside Fernsby, where she finally burst into tears.

FERNSBY RANTED and cursed all the way back to Thornwood Hall.

"I will blast him to Hades and back. I will kill him myself with my own bare hands and have him clapped into Newgate for the rest of his life. No, even better. I will disinherit him, ha! Let him see how he likes that.

The audacity to frighten an old man so! I swear I have aged twenty years these past few hours and will never recover from this scare."

After they'd identified Syd Barker's body, a man had stepped up to them and explained that the body of the ginger-bearded man was that of his colleague, a fellow runner from Bow Street. It turned out that the place was swarming with runners.

"They've sent the entire Bow Street force here," the innkeeper grumbled, then happily supplied them with beer.

After Avery had swooned, a man in a black coat entered, introducing himself as a constable.

"This is Jake Winslow," he said, pointing to the unidentified body. "He was fatally shot in the ensuing struggle while trying to capture Syd Barker."

"One thing at a time," Fernsby put in. "Lady Avery, sit down here and have a glass of wine. It will revive your spirits. And you, don't run away," he barked at the man. "Tell me, where is Blackshurst?"

"I believe his lordship had to return urgently to Bow Street to oversee the next course of action. I must say we all admire his lordship very much. It was a highly dangerous operation, and he conducted himself with great courage. We are very fortunate to have such an intrepid superintendent."

"Superintendent?" Avery breathed.

Fernsby knitted his brow. "You speak as if Blackshurst were some sort of authority on the matter."

"Certainly, sir. He has been our superior for the last decade or so. He's well respected for training the runners and working closely with the Home Office in reforming the police system. Thanks to him and his extensive knowledge of highwaymen, we have been able to root out not only the dreaded Esher gang, but also the gang around Syd Barker. The man has eluded us for two decades. Thanks to the brilliance of Blackshurst, the era of highwaymen terrorising Hounslow Heath is finally over."

"Bring me some tea. No. I need something stronger. A whisky," Fernsby called to the innkeeper. "And you, tell us from the beginning, in order. What exactly happened? And leave no detail out."

"Blackshurst sent out an urgent summons to Bow Street last night, asking for reinforcements to apprehend Syd Barker. He knew from unidentified sources that he'd be staying here at the inn and hereabouts. We arrived well after midnight, no doubt taking him by surprise because he'd taken up residence here with three other gang members. We surrounded the inn and ordered them to surrender. He attempted to take the innkeeper hostage, overlooking the fact that Blackshurst had managed to sneak into the inn through the coal cellar. We broke in through the front door and there was a wild fight in the tavern. My poor colleague here was shot in the melee. Blackshurst cornered Syd Barker and told him to give himself up to the law. The man laughed and threw himself at Blackshurst, saying he wanted to fight to the death. He tried to wrestle the gun from Blackshurst's hand but only managed to get himself shot. The rest of the gang surrendered, and Blackshurst himself took them to gaol."

"So now he's a Bow Street runner on top of every-thing else." That was the only comment Avery found herself capable of uttering. "Not even that. A superinten-dent, you said?"

"His Lordship is to be our next chief magistrate in Bow Street, as Sampson Wright, our present magistrate, thinks very highly of him."

"Chief magistrate." Fernsby wiped his hand over his face. His shoulders began to shake. He laughed. Then he cursed, and he did not stop cursing until they were back at Thornwood Hall.

Avery stayed quiet all the way back. When they arrived at the hall, she turned to Fernsby and told him she wanted to go back to London.

Fernsby knitted his brow. "Jax will expect you to stay here. Those were his explicit instructions, I believe."

She straightened her spine. "Yes, without consulting me first. I can't possibly sit here and twiddle my thumbs waiting for him to return. I have much to do. I would be grateful if you could arrange a carriage for me. I must go home."

She needed to be alone.

To think.

To unravel her heated thoughts.

Fernsby protested a little more, then gave in to her request when he saw she was determined to return.

He held her hand longer than usual. "It has been a harrowing morning for both of us, and I dare say you need some solitude to process the recent events. I will see to it that you are transported safely to your home in London. You are quite right not to wait for Jax to finish his business. Are you very displeased with him, my lady?"

Avery shook her head. "Yes. No. Oh, I don't know! I just need to return home and think. I need to write some letters." And she desperately needed some perspective on her life.

Chapter Thirty

WHEN AVERY RETURNED TO WIMPOLE STREET, FRED the footman opened the door and beamed at her.

"Is Jerkins in?" Avery asked as she pulled the gloves off her hands.

"No, my lady, he has been on leave of absence for the last few days."

"Leave of absence. Well, that's new." She looked at the trunks and suitcases in the hall. "And whose are they?"

"They belong to Lord Blackshurst, my lady." His face remained impassive, and he spoke without batting an eyelid, as if he found it nothing out of the ordinary that Blackshurst and Jerkins were one and the same person. "He has announced that he is moving out of The Clarendon and back to his townhouse."

"I see. I shall be in the study, Fred, and not available to callers, should there be any."

"Yes, my lady. Lady Jersey has called twice. Mrs Wimplethorpe is currently visiting with Her Ladyship."

Avery sighed.

She locked herself in the study, sat down at the desk, and stared at her half-finished manuscript. She picked it up, went to the fireplace, and threw the whole thing into the fire, watching it crackle and burn. She felt relief seeing it burn, for the story had been one-dimensional and overly simplistic. It was symbolic of her life and how it had been before she'd fallen in love with Jerkins. Yet as she watched the paper reduce to ashes, she felt sadness, for it had been her first story ever, however mangled and badly written it was.

What a dreadful state of affairs this was!

Love, that is.

She should have thought twice before putting 'falling in love' on her Never List. Naturally, she had to go and fall in love with a highly complicated man who seemed to be unable to commit to the sentiment, regardless of what Fernsby had told her at Thornwood Hall. He would love and worship her, but only from afar.

A bleak sense of desolation washed through her.

Why were none of the men whom she loved in her life present and capable of being there for her?

There was her father, who'd abandoned her by dying. He'd loved her but had failed to provide for her future. Her brother, who'd always taken her presence for granted, who'd never really seen her and never would. And now Blackshurst, who claimed to love her, but when it came down to it, could not commit to his true feelings for her.

It would put her in danger, he'd said.

A sad smile stole onto her face.

He'd been so wrong. She'd put him in danger, and he'd nearly lost his life.

But if she had the chance, would she do it all over again? Would she make the same decisions? Would she fall in love again?

"Yes," she whispered to herself. Every time.

Then she returned to her desk, took out a fresh sheet of paper and a pen, and, after a short pause, began to write.

AVERY WROTE all day and all night.

Just before the first grey rays of dawn crept through the window, she wrote with a flourish, 'The End.'

She read it over and thought it was good.

She placed it in the middle of the desk.

After a moment's hesitation, she wrote: *To Jax Tyrrell, Thief of Hearts.*

Then, before she could change her mind, she rang the bell.

"Order a carriage, please. And ask the servants to gather in the hall."

Her things were packed quickly. She had only one small bag to carry a dress, a second pair of shoes, and her reticule.

When she opened the drawer of her dressing table, she found her bracelet.

Jerkins had never pawned it as she'd asked him to.

With a lump in her throat, she fastened it around her wrist.

She wrote a quick note and addressed it to Belinda. She would not have time to say good-bye to her in person.

Then she went downstairs where the servants were waiting for her.

"Now that Lord Blackshurst is officially returning to his home, as he rightly should, it would be highly inappropriate for me to take advantage of his hospitality and stay longer. The time for me has come to remove myself to Dorset. Please tell Mrs Wimplethorpe that I have had to leave urgently." She handed Fred her note. "I wish to thank you all for your service." Avery's voice wavered. She swallowed as she held out her hand to Emma, who burst into tears. "I will miss you all."

She pulled Emma into her arms.

She shook hands with everyone and found herself missing Jerkins sorely.

Jerkins, with his bulky grey wig and humorous grey eyes gleaming behind his glasses.

Jerkins, who had been so safe.

Jerkins, who did not exist.

She wiped away the memories with a determined gesture of her hand and climbed into her carriage.

IT HAD BEEN A GRAND ADVENTURE, Avery thought.

She opened her tapestry bag and pulled out a sheet of paper: her Never List.

She'd accomplished almost everything she'd written on the list.

She'd had a Season. She'd danced through the night. She'd had an exciting adventure.

She'd fallen in love.

She put the list down and leaned her head against the wall of the carriage.

And oh, how she'd fallen! With everything she had, with every fibre of her soul. A dreamy smile played on her lips. How glorious it was to love.

There was nothing more wonderful, nor more painful in life.

She looked at her list and tore it into little pieces. Then she opened the window and let them fly.

The little pieces of paper fluttered in the air and flew up into the sky.

She would write stories, Avery vowed. Lots of them. She would read them to Great-Aunt Euphemia, and on the long, cold winter evenings she would smile as she recalled a dashing highwayman, a loyal butler, and a rakish lord, all with the same humorous twinkle in their steel-grey eyes.

The monotonous rattling of the carriage caused Avery to doze off. Having stayed up all night, she was beyond exhausted.

A clap of thunder woke her. The sky was dark, even though it was the middle of the day.

A thunderstorm.

She looked out of the window and wondered why the weather insisted on being bad every time she crossed Hounslow Heath.

Another clap of thunder made her jump in her seat.

This one had been very close.

"Stand and deliver!" An imperious voice lashed out.

The coach came to a halt, and in the silence that descended, she could hear the horses panting.

The carriage door was thrown open, and she found herself staring down the barrel of a pistol.

Avery squeezed her eyes shut. Blast, she had forgotten her pistol, she thought before opening her eyes again. She glared at the dark figure looming in the carriage doorway.

"I have no valuables," she informed him. "Unless you care for a threadbare dress, a purse with five shillings in it, and oh—I suppose I have this." She unfastened the bracelet from her wrist and held it up. "Will that do?"

"You have something much more valuable," the man said in a muffled voice, for he wore a mask over his eyes, and his mouth was covered by a scarf.

"Really? I can't imagine what it could be."

He swung into the carriage and closed the door.

Avery looked out. "Are you alone? I have it on good authority that highwaymen can't properly plunder a coach when they're alone. And judging by the way you're going about it, you're not doing a proper job," she informed him.

The highwayman laughed hollowly, reached out, and pulled her onto his lap. She clung to the lapels of his coat.

"You should just let me go," she told him sadly.

"Never. I have come to claim what is mine."

She began to struggle. "I wish you would stop. Just stop! Is this a game to you? Are you doing this because you enjoy it? Because, sir, let me tell you, I do not."

She was crying.

He held her to his chest, rocking her back and forth as if she were a small child. "Shh."

"We thought you were dead," she sniffled. "We were called to the inn to identify your body." She cried harder.

He pressed his still-covered mouth to her head. "I know. I am so terribly sorry you had to go through that. The whole thing was a disaster, and we lost a good man. Somehow, in the confusion, word got out that it was me. Don't ask me how. And I suppose the news reached Thornwood Hall before it could be corrected."

"Fernsby nearly had a stroke." Avery tugged at his scarf and pulled it away. She wanted to see his mouth. "The poor man."

"I know. I have never seen him so angry. He would never have forgiven me if I had died, and then he could hardly forgive me for not dying. He disinherited me twice and reinstated me once. I am not certain of my current status as his heir."

"Why couldn't you have told me earlier that you were working for Bow Street all this time? Why the charade?"

"I didn't want anyone to know, Avery. I needed to be in town, I needed Blackshurst to be abroad, I needed to be undercover, and so I rented my townhouse. The identity of a butler proved convenient, and it occurred to me that I could stay in town in my own house if I pretended to be my own butler. It seemed to work for the most part when I rented the house to a Mr George Shelton. He was old and slept most of the day. After he died, your brother expressed interest in the house, and you moved in. And then when your brother left for the Continent, the idea was that the butler would disappear and Blackshurst would return for good. Imagine my surprise when you turned up that night and insisted on staying." He grinned. "Within a month, you had uncovered Blackshurst and Jax Tyrrell's identities. You are amazing."

She pulled the mask from his eyes. "When I saw you at St Giles that day, what were you doing there?"

"I was briefing the runners on our next move. We were working undercover and getting close to Syd Barker, but he kept evading us."

"You allowed me to stay in your house and put up with my antics. You did not have to appear as Lord Blackshurst and dance with me, or save me from that gambling disaster, but you did."

"You were a terrible distraction, yes. But a lovable one. And to my surprise, you did what none of us in Bow Street was capable of accomplishing: you coaxed Syd Barker out of hiding and straight to our house. That break-in? He left his mark, of course. I recognised his weapon at once. All he took was a bottle of my cologne, which he soon used to lure you in."

"It worked because when I went to Vauxhall Gardens, I thought he was you."

He growled. "An unforgivable mistake."

"You used me as bait."

"I didn't. I wanted you to be safe, and I wanted you to trust me. Which you stubbornly refused to do." He shook his head. "When he took you, I was out of my mind with worry."

"Then we're even," Avery whispered. "Because I aged a decade when they announced you had died in the shooting."

He leaned his forehead against hers.

"And now what?" she whispered.

"And now, Lady Avery, it is my turn to kidnap you. Because I will not allow you to leave."

"I must return to the ground of reality. I have family responsibilities. I have an aunt to look after." Her mind whirled. "I am too much of a danger to you."

"I want you to return with me."

"Why?" Her eyes brimmed with tears.

"Because I have loved you ever since you set foot in my house three years ago. You never even noticed me. I was just the butler, was I not? Yet I watched over you, and I realised you are a most kind-hearted person, gentle and tender with your little rascals, in possession of a marvellous imagination. I used to love listening to your stories from behind the door. And it was because of you that I decided to let Fothergill stay on longer in the house than was necessary so I could be near you yet still keep a safe distance. Then your brother went to the Continent, and you left for Dorset. Letting you go was the hardest thing I have ever had to do in my life, and I swore I'd never do it again. Avery, my life is not all roses and romance. I deal with criminals, crime, and danger. It is not something the polite society looks on favourably. It is a sordid occupation."

"What are you saying?" she whispered.

"I'm asking you to marry me, Avery. But it would not be a life in high society. We could travel a bit if you like, but afterwards I will spend more time in Bow Street than in the ballrooms. It might end up rather dull for you."

"I'd be in the study writing stories," She smiled at him through a veil of tears.

"Ah, yes. I read the story you left on the desk. It is very well done."

"Did you like it?" Avery wiped her cheeks with the handkerchief he gave her.

"Of course I did. Just one little detail you might want to correct..." His eyes danced.

"Oh, do be quiet!" Avery placed her hand over his mouth. "Be quiet and kiss me."

"I'll take that as a yes to my proposal." He crushed her against him and claimed her lips.

"What about Great-Aunt Euphemia?" she murmured afterwards.

"How about we send the coach to fetch her?"

"Oh, do you think we could? That would make me feel so much better. I feel terrible for having neglected her all this time."

He glanced at the sky, where the storm had temporarily abated. "I shall have to kidnap you, then, so we can make it to Thornwood Hall before nightfall, where Fernsby is anxiously awaiting us."

Avery snuggled into his arms and sighed contentedly. "Oh, yes, I would very much like to be kidnapped, Jerkins, Jax, Julius. We really must decide on one name, only."

Epilogue

"Have you heard? The Black Earl has finally been caught in parson's mousetrap," whispered one lady to another.

The lady slowly waved her peacock fan. "Indeed. I read the announcement in the *Morning Gazette*." She tapped her fan against her pursed lips. "A shame. It really is. They say she's a nobody. An old spinster, can you imagine? The sister of that diplomat. I forget his name."

"It's Lord Fothergill," replied another lady to the right. A purple feather bounced above her dark curls.

"Ah, yes. That one. A mystery how she managed to catch him when none of the others could. They say he had hundreds of lovers."

"Three hundred and sixty-seven, I heard," a third lady in a mustard-yellow dress chimed in. It made her skin look pale.

"Shocking. Really! Absolutely shocking," sniffed the lady with the peacock fan.

"But Lady Comingham, I recall you threw your own

daughter in his way to encourage a match, so you need not be so utterly shocked," put in the lady with the purple feather.

Lady Comingham's cheeks flushed a dull red. "You must be mistaken. I would never want one of my daughters to marry a rake, least of all the Black Earl. One could not wish for anything more unfortunate to happen to one's daughter."

"And you, Lady Dawson, did you not flirt with him yourself at Lady Jersey's ball?"

"Certainly not," Lady Dawson said with a stiff upper lip.

The lady in the mustard-yellow gown took out her quizzing glass and examined the outspoken lady with the purple feather.

"I don't think we've been introduced," she said in an icy tone, ready to give her the cut.

The lady with the purple feather tapped the arm of a lady in white who was standing nearby, talking to a group of people. "Lady Jersey, would you mind introducing me to this group of ladies?"

"Certainly. Lady Comingham, Lady Dawson, and Lady Wetherby. This is Mrs Belinda Wimplethorpe."

The ladies nodded frostily.

"She is the cousin of my dear friend, the new Countess of Blackshurst," Lady Jersey added.

There was silence as Belinda beamed at them.

Lady Jersey looked up. "And here they are. Well met."

The Earl of Blackshurst and his newly married wife stood at the entrance of the ballroom. The earl looked as striking as ever in his full-dress black evening attire. And Lady Avery was lovely in a cherry-red silk organza ball-room gown, with trimming down the middle and on the sleeves. She looked eagerly about the ballroom, fanning her face.

Belinda rushed to Avery's side and curtsied. "My lady. My lord. May I congratulate you on your marriage? Avery, you look wonderful, like a rose."

"Thank you, Belinda. But goodness! We need not stand on such ceremony. And I can't thank you enough for being our witness at the wedding this morning."

"Oh, mind you, it is not for your benefit, but for those who are watching." She lowered her voice. "You are the talk of the town."

"Finally." Avery grinned. "It's on my Never List, you see. I decided to make another one."

Blackshurst, who had been talking to Lady Jersey, looked up and smiled. "If you will excuse me, I must spirit my wife away for the waltz."

"Oh, but it is rather ill-mannered to dance with one's wife when there is a room full of other women to choose from!" exclaimed Lady Jersey.

He gave her a smile. "Lady Jersey. The only woman I will dance with from now on is my wife."

"No longer a rogue, I see." She smiled indulgently.

As Blackshurst drew Avery into his arms, he murmured into her hair, "Why are we here again? Remind me."

"To let society see us together as a newlywed couple. To establish Blackshurst's reputation as a firmly happily married man."

He glanced at his pocket watch. "We said only an hour. We'll be in Dover by that time tomorrow."

"And then on to Paris." She lifted her bright eyes to his. "Vienna, Venice, Florence, and Rome. It will be a fabulous honeymoon. I can't wait; I've never been to those cities. And so many things to cross off my Never List!"

"My love. There are many more Nevers we can explore together." His eyes twinkled.

She tilted her head to the side. "Such as?"

"Let yourself be surprised."

A collective gasp went through the ballroom as he kissed her full on the mouth in the middle of the waltz.

* * *

WHEN A PROUD BEAUTY weds a humble costermonger, their worlds collide with challenges and secrets that only love can conquer.

Don't miss Louisa's story in the next instalment of the Merry Spinsters, Charming Rogues series: Miss Louisa's Final Waltz.

Also by Sofi Laporte

The Wishing Well Series:

Lucy and the Duke of Secrets

Arabella and the Reluctant Duke

Birdie and the Beastly Duke

Penelope and the Wicked Duke

A Christmas Regency Novella:

A Mistletoe Promise

Wishing Well Seminary Series:

Miss Hilversham and the Pesky Duke

Merry Spinsters, Charming Rogues:

Lady Ludmilla's Accidental Letter

Miss Ava's Scandalous Secret

Lady Avery and the False Butler

Miss Louisa's Final Waltz

About the Author

Sofi was born in Vienna, grew up in Seoul, studied Comparative Literature in Maryland, U.S.A., and lived in Quito with her Ecuadorian husband. When not writing, she likes to scramble about the countryside exploring medieval castle ruins. She currently lives with her husband, 3 trilingual children, a sassy cat and a cheeky dog in Europe.

Get in touch and visit Sofi at her Website, on Facebook or Instagram!

amazon.com/Sofi-Laporte/e/Bo7N1K8H6C

facebook.com/sofilaporteauthor

instagram.com/sofilaporteauthor

bookbub.com/profile/sofi-laporte